T0194575

THE REALTOR

MAY'LON "MAZE" MIRANDA

authorHOUSE®

AuthorHouse™
1663 Liberty Drive
Bloomington, IN 47403
www.authorhouse.com
Phone: 1 (800) 839-8640

Published by AuthorHouse   03/04/2019

ISBN: 978-1-7283-0285-0 (sc)
ISBN: 978-1-7283-0284-3 (e)

Print information available on the last page.

This Book is Dedicated to the Loving
Memory of Louis and Anna Miranda
I love and miss you both.
R.I.P.

This Book was Inspired by a DREAM
Always DREAM and THINK BIG. DREAMS are
All we have.........Nobody can take them from us.

- Author May'lon "Maze" Miranda

I WOKE UP IN THIS DARK room I couldn't see anything at all and had know idea where I was at or what had happened to me. All I could hear was water running like a leaky pipe had been running or something like that. I was so scared my hands were tied to the arms of a chair as were my feet as well. The place smelled old and musty like it hadn't been used or cleaned in years. As I yelled, "Help!!!!!! Help!!!!! please somebody help me!!!!!!!!!!" crying hysterically.

I felt as if I had sat in that chair for hours but nobody came for me because I was cramped up from sitting down for so long. The windows were all covered up so I couldn't tell whether it was day or night much less where I was at. I screamed and I yelled until I couldn't possibly yell or scream anymore because my throat became swollen and achy from yelling so much. Then all of a sudden I hear footsteps approaching as the footsteps became closer and closer as I yelled again,

"Help me!!!!! Please!!!!! Help!!!! in here!!!! in here!!!!, I'm in here!!!." I could hear a door open and the lights turn on and I'm in what appears to be a basement or cellar of some sort maybe even a shed. In comes the foot steps closer and closer but my eyes are blurred by the bright lights and the tears from the hours of crying while sitting in the dark. As the person came closer and closer I was so happy and relieved to see that it was Bernie my Realtor. I noticed that it was him because Bernie was very tall and slim, he was built like a basketball player and wore a very bad smelling cheap cologne. He also walked very funny as I yelled,

"Thank god!!!!!", Bernie please help me where am I?"

"Shhhhh!!!!" Bernie replied.

"Calm down it's ok, everything is going to be ok I am here now."

"Thank god please untie me Bernie what happened? Where am I?" "What do you mean where are you at silly? You don't remember where you are at? Bernie replied laughing.

"No I don't, what is so funny?" I replied.

"There is nothing funny about this Bernie." I continued to say "Where is Craig at?"

"Now, now, now there is no need to get so serious, I found you didn't I? And Craig well Craig I was wondering the same thing? You know, I came by to bring you over some more of my famous lemonade that you like so much and I noticed that your front door was cracked open. He continued,

"That is very dangerous, anybody could have walked in so if anything you should be glad that it was me and not a stranger Olivia you are lucky to be alive."

"I'm in my house? What are you talking about? You came by? I'm lucky to be alive? This is not my house what is wrong with you? Fucking untie me dammit."

"Shhhh" listen Olivia, this is very important. I need you to try and think real hard about what you remember happened to you? Anything you can tell me please? I can't help you unless you help me."

"What the fuck are you talking about? I don't remember anything I was at home watching television, I got tired, I fell asleep, and woke up here, please untie me and let me go." Olivia replied.

"Ok let me find something to untie you with."

As he goes off looking for something I noticed that Bernie was dressed like he had been at work. He was in a nice suit and tie but by the time he came back into the room just a few minutes later he was wearing a black T-shirt and a pair of jeans. He closed the door behind him and walked over to an old dirty table with a cloth over some objects. When he removed the cloth he says,

"Oh here goes somethings to untie you with."

"Oh my god, you did this to me you sick fuck why?" As I screamed.

It was a table full of knives, bats, guns, you name it. As the look on his face turned from helpful to harmful in a matter of seconds. Because at first he looked like the Bernie I was first introduced to when we purchased the place, but the look on his face was scary almost like it was a completely different person a satanic look I was so scared. I plead with him,

"Please let me go" what do you want from me? I plead with him.

"What do you mean what do I want?" Bernie replied laughing sickly. He continued,

"I want you to be my first."

3

"You're a sick fuck I would never sleep with you not in a million years!" I said.

"That is completely fine by me Olivia because you see nobody but me knows you're here which means time is all you have so a million years, a month, a week, it really depends on you when you leave here." Bernie continued,

"Olivia it really doesn't matter to me don't you want to see Craig again? I can send you back to him with a few new tricks."

"Fuck you! You'd have to kill me first. I replied.

"Oh I plan on it." Bernie replied.

"Please Bernie don't kill me, why are you doing this to me?" As I began to cry.

"Honestly, no reason at all. You see you and your faggot boyfriend seem like really nice people it's a simple case of the wrong place at the wrong time." Bernie replied.

"You see mommy and daddy didn't abuse me, I didn't come from a broken home, in fact I grew up great with all the privileges in the world. What it comes down to sweetheart is that I just love to see that look you know the look right? The look before they know that they are about to die. Like they know it's coming as the knife pierces their skin and seeps in and they know they are about to die? Well I live for that look, I live for that feeling and well I'm not going to lie to you Olivia, you are going to die whether that is today or in a million years from now as you put it." Bernie continued.

"Your either going to do what I ask you to do or I will keep you here for as long as I want to and once I get tired of you refusing me I will fucking kill you bitch and you ask me why?, Well the answer is simple my dear, it's because I can.

Does that answer all of your questions for you? I'm going to kill you and my only regret is that I only get to do it once."

"How did I get here?" I replied crying hysterically.

"Well sweety, my lemonade is famous and you just had too much that's all and that's all I will tell you about that so final question?" Bernie replied.

"Have you hurt Craig?"

"No you're little boyfriend is perfectly fine but he won't be for long your wasting time Olivia. So I tell you what I'll let you walk out of here right now all you have to do is suck my dick what do you say?"

"You are insane you know that?" I replied crying.

"You know what, you could be right but nevertheless I'm free, you're not so is that a refusal I take it? Maybe I should go visit Craig and make him do it although I'd prefer you and those gorgeous lips" As he laughed.

"Fuck you! You're sick."

"Ok have it your way see you tomorrow Olivia." As he walked towards the door to exit,

"No wait, please" Crying heavily.

"I'll do it".

Bernie slowly turned back around from the door facing me,

"You will do what Olivia?"

"I will do what you want me to do, please just don't hurt me or Craig." I replied.

"What is it exactly that you will do Olivia? I want to hear you say it, tell me what you want to do to me baby?" Feeling so nasty, so disgusted, and, repulsed by his sickness I replied,

"I will suck your dick". Bernie replied

"See now was that so hard no pun intended? I mean you were going to make me kill you over that? Hell I was going to make your boyfriend do it imagine how mad he would have been at you for making him do that shit huh?" Laughing he continued,

"Alright great let's get to it."

"How do I know after I do this you won't kill me anyways"? I asked.

"That is a good question and the answer is quite frankly that you don't, however I am a man of my word and if I tell you that I'm going to let you go and that I wont kill you or your boyfriend I won't." He continued.

"But there's just one other stipulation and that is that nobody and I mean nobody will ever know about what took place here today which means you take this to your grave. You don't tell a soul not the police, not your boyfriend, not your parents, friends, nobody, and in return I will guarantee the safety of you and Craig you will never ever see me again after today as long as you keep your mouth shut. But if you don't, I will come back find you and him torture and kill you both oh and as an insurance policy don't move do you understand these simple rules to the game I've given you?"

"I do, please don't kill me Bernie please."

"You have my word Olivia." Bernie replied.

"Let's get this over with you sick fuck." I replied crying hysterically.

Bernie now walks over to the dirty table and picks up a gun. "Help!!!!!, help!!!!!, somebody help!!!!! I began screaming.

"Nobody can hear you bitch shut the fuck up I'm not going to kill you this is just so that you do your job right. Bernie replied laughing.

As Bernie walks up to me and places the gun to my head, as I try to move from out the way of the gun,

"Stay still bitch" he says.

"Calm down, I'm not going to shoot you this is simply so that you know not to even fucking think of biting me because if you bite me I will pull the trigger do you understand?"

"Yes I understand that you're a sick twisted fuck." I replied.

Bernie began to unzipper his pants as I began to vomit everywhere.

"Now see what you did, you dumb fucking whore? He continues.

"You are starting to piss me off now bitch. Look I'm going to clean this up and get you mouth wash or water or something I will be right back dammit."

I can remember the sick feeling that I felt when he came back in the room with a cloth and a cup of water in his hand I kept feeling myself getting more and more nauseous by the seconds.

"Ok are you ready now Olivia?" Crying with vomit all over my white T-shirt, I replied,

"Yes let's get this over with you fucking psycho."

"Great!, now open your mouth and don't try any funny stuff or like I said I will blow your fucking brains all over this place and Craig will be next so you better do a good job and make me cum." Bernie began to unzipper his pants and remove his penis from his jean pants. I was so repulsed by what I saw that I was about to vomit again but I was trying so hard not to because I was sure that if I did again he would kill me for sure. As he got closer and closer to me holding his penis with his left hand and holding a gun in his right he placed the gun on the left side of my head while he placed his nasty, disgusting, dirty, penis to my mouth and told me to open up wide. I have never been in my life so scared and humiliated and yet this sick fuck was so comfortable almost as if he had done this type of thing before as I'm sure he had. So I closed my eyes and opened my mouth as he placed his penis in my mouth and instructed me on how he wanted it done. Bernie kept saying

"Suck it nice and slow" Bernie kept saying.

"Tell me how bad of a slut you are?" As I closed my eyes and just cried and cried.

"Stop crying you whore don't act like you haven't done this before just pretend I'm Craig just with a bigger dick of course that is."

"Open your eyes Olivia" he said, but I ignored him and just kept going. Then I heard the gun cock.

"Open your eyes slut now and tell me that your daddy's little cunt" and that you love being a nasty little whore or I'm going to shoot you in the fucking face as he drops the gun from my head to the side of my face. He continued.

As I continued sucking, he pulled his penis from out my mouth and said repeat what I just told you to say.

"I'm daddy's little cunt and I love being a nasty little whore." Crying, I replied.

"Aww yeah baby that's right," As he placed his penis back into my mouth and began stroking. His moans grew louder and louder as tears ran down my face I could feel him about to explode in my mouth as I began choking and turning red. He told me

"Awww baby keep going faster and faster." As I felt a warm rush of salt water burst into my mouth I stopped and began vomiting all over the floor and coughing up a lung as Bernie was pale in the face and said,

"Ok clean up Olivia get it together."

"Fuck you Bernie let me go you sick fucking bastard!"

"Oh my god that was good Olivia" let me get cleaned up and I will get you cleaned up as well and then you are free to go I promise a deal is a deal ok?"

Bernie then turned around and left out the room. When he came back in, he was back in his suit and tie and began cleaning my face and mouth with a washcloth.

"Ok well I am done with you Miss. Olivia and you remember what I told you right? You keep your end of the bargain or I will find you and Craig and kill you both it's not like I don't know where you both live at." As he began laughing like a crazy person.

"As for me, I will keep mine I'm letting you go and I will be getting lost you will never see me again. Now drink this tea and this will all have seemed like one big nightmare and you will end up back in your living room on your couch."

"You told me that I was home Bernie?" Bernie replied

"You are home Olivia." Bernie replied.

"Then why can't you just untie me and let me go?"

"Because that is not how I want to end this date now hurry up and drink it Olivia you are wasting precious time."

"You need help" I replied as I downed Bernie's famous tea.

"As it kicks in really fast you begin to feel very light headed in a weird way it was a good drunken feeling only that it hits you way to fast." He added.

I remember feeling very dizzy, light headed, and I must of passed out or something because Bernie kept his promise and I woke up right back on my couch as if nothing ever happened. Was this maybe all just a bad dream I said to myself? The first thing I did when I came out of it a little bit was call my boyfriend Craig to make sure that he was ok. I remember calling him.

"Baby is everything alright? You sound panicked? Craig asked.

"No everything is ok babe, I guess I just had a really bad nightmare but you are ok right?"

"Yeah babe why wouldn't I be? I'm here at work filing paper work with the Professor you must of just had a really bad nightmare. I'm fine how's everything at the house?"

"Umm yeah you're probably right everything is great over here I must of fell asleep on the couch or something I'm going to get back to unpacking and what not ok babe? Sorry to bother you at work." I replied.

"Not a problem at all I love hearing your voice baby, now I'm going to get back to work I love you and will talk to you in a few ok? Craig continued.

"I love you too, ok babe talk to you later bye" I replied and we hung up. I was so confused that couldn't have been a dream I kept saying to myself that was real where was I at? Think Olivia think? I was trying to remember what had first had happened to me from the very beginning but it was blank. Like I remember sitting down watching television but maybe I was watching a horror flick? Why my front door was cracked open? He claims it was? He said I was home? So I began looking around the house to see if there were any doors that lead to other rooms but where could it be? This was only a two bedroom home a nice looking place right off of campus.

My boyfriend and I attends UCLA. My name is Olivia Math and my boyfriend is Craig. We were new to California and had only been attending UCLA for a little over a year. I was going for my bachelor's degree in nursing and my boyfriend Craig was on a scholarship for football but also to make ends meet filed papers from time to time after school hours for the Professor and made some extra cash doing so. He and I both got tired of living with roommates on campus and decided to get a house together off of campus. Craig is so good to me and always wanted me to have the best so he left things completely in my hands as far as finding the perfect affordable home for us to live in while he worked. We are both born and raised in Las Vegas, Nevada he was the star quarterback for Eastside High School and I was the prom queen every year to his king. I was a student at Eastside High School but I wasn't Barbie and he wasn't ken I was very intelligent and so was he. We weren't your average prom king and queen, bimbo and jock, we were the new age popular kids by new age I mean smart. Anyways after weeks and weeks of searching for the perfect place I finally found this really nice two bedroom, one bathroom, house right off of campus I was so excited about it and couldn't wait to tell Craig about it. I found it through a real estate agency called Master Reality Company and the owner and head agent Realtor's name was

"Bernie" Burke Walters. We had spoken over the phone a few times and the place online looked beautiful and the price was very affordable as well. I couldn't wait to tell Craig about it and even more excited about going to actually see it in person. When I finally told Craig about it I think he was just as happy to see how happy that I was to have finally found one because I had been driving him crazy about a place for weeks. What color should it be? Where should it be? You know the typical woman nagging and my boyfriend Craig was all about his football and left everything as far as moving in my hands and what not which made it very overwhelming for me and then I would put a lot on him. So he was thrilled that I found one I remember the day we went to go see the house we met up with Mr. Walters outside of the beautiful home. Mr. Walters pulled up in a brand new 2011 Mercedes-Benz S500 all black and beautiful. He stepped out the car in a black blazer dress suit with his jet black hair slicked back he was the tall dark handsome looking type. He was a very nice older gentleman he showed us all around the home but before he did that he introduced himself like this he said,

"Hi you must be Olivia we spoke on the phone a few times? My name is Walter Burke but all my friends all me Bernie".

"Well it is nice to finally meet you in person Bernie and yes my name is Olivia and this is my boyfriend Craig." I replied.

"Well it is nice to meet you both" as he shook both of our hands.

"Let's get right into it and show you both this beautiful home" Bernie said.

"It is a nice two bedroom home with one bath perfect for a couple such as yourselves the university is literally around the corner. Bernie continues.

"It's spacious and close to just about everything trust me when I tell you that for college students you can't possibly beat or do any better than this."

"Yeah it is a really nice place and it beats living on campus so baby if you like it I'm all for it. Craig replied.

"Baby I love it I really do but can we afford it?" I asked.

"You let me worry about that babe." Craig continued."

"Ok well Mr. Walters it is right? I'm sorry? Asked Craig.

"Walter Burke actually but just call me Bernie." Bernie replied.

"Forgive me for that my bad, I'm bad with names I'm sorry about that. Craig replied.

"That is quite ok." Bernie replied.

"Ok well let's do this we will take it. Craig continued.

"Great I will draw up the paper work and I will meet you both back here tomorrow around shall we say 4:00 pm?" Bernie asked.

"Yes, that sounds great!" as I looked over at Craig and said,

"I am so happy oh my god baby we have our own place."

"Yes that's great babe I am happy too but tomorrow after school I have practice so do you mind handling this alone? Craig asked.

"Well we can always reschedule?" asked Bernie.

"No, no, no," that's fine, Olivia will meet you here at 4:00 pm tomorrow ok? Craig replied.

"Are you sure because it's really not a problem? Bernie asked.

"No, I know how much this means to my baby we will handle it all tomorrow." Craig replied.

"Well ok then it was nice meeting you Craig and Olivia I guess I will see you tomorrow at 4:00 pm then and congratulations to the both of you thank you." Bernie said. Craig and I replied,

"No, thank you very much."

"You are both very welcome have a nice day." Bernie replied. And we all went our separate ways.

The next day, I believe it was on a Thursday, I couldn't wait until 4:00. I was so excited and was bragging to all my family and friends about how Craig and I just got our own place. Not an apartment but a house It was just unreal to me I was so excited and happy about it all. Once around 3:30 came, I was getting ready to go meet up with Bernie, now by the time 4:00 came we had both been pulling up to the house at the same time and I noticed that Bernie had got out of his vehicle with his briefcase and a jar of some sort. When he approached just as he was about to drop it he passed it off to me,

"I am so sorry I almost dropped it", he said.

"That is for you, it's my famous lemonade you will love it. Look at it as a house warming gift if you may. Every time I make a sale, I give some to my customers and they all say the same thing." He added.

"Oh wow thank you and what is that?" I asked.

"That it's to die for". He said.

Something seemed very odd about Bernie to me I just couldn't put my finger on it. Anyways, we went into the house and he presented me with all the proper legal documents which I reviewed then signed and as a result of that I was now the proud new owner of our first home with key in hand and might I add it felt good very good. As a toast, Bernie was excited for me to try his lemonade which was odd. So when I opened it to have a try,

"Well silly me, there are no cups."

"Well I hope this doesn't seem strange to you but I brought one glass for us." Bernie replied.

"Oh wow," do you always carry a glass with you? I asked.

"Oh no, now that would just be weird," laughing nervously still and continued,

"No, I bring lemonade and a glass as a toast when I sell a home." Bernie said.

"Oh ok, well why do you only have one glass if there are two of us here?" I asked.

"Good question, well I don't drink lemonade and I knew that your boyfriend wasn't able to make it here today." Bernie replied.

"Oh ok so you wanted me to toast by myself?" I asked Bernie with complete confusion.

Still laughing nervously he says,

"Of course not, silly I have a can of soda for myself dear."

"Right yeah silly me" I replied.

"Wait, why do you make lemonade if you don't drink it? Now no offense but that is a little weird don't you think?" I asked Bernie.

"Can I tell you a little story?" Bernie replied.

"Um yeah sure I guess." I replied.

"Trust me, this won't take long." Bernie said.

"So there was this guy who met this girl. The guy was in real estate and the girl was a farmer. She took after her father so she loved to plant all sorts of fruits and vegetables. Anyways her favorite thing was lemons to squeeze them when it was time so that she could make lemonade and drink it quite often. So as time went by, she taught this young real estate agent how to plant and make lemonade. A few years down, the line that girl dies of cancer so this young real estate agent only remembered good times and memories of toasting to her lemonade after it was planted then made, but after she died he vowed that he would never drink it again but simply make it to toast on behalf of others joys or fortunes in her memory.

"Oh my god, Bernie I am so sorry I didn't know I'm sorry."

"Well it's quite alright lets toast to your new home." Bernie replied.

"Let's do that, cheers." As I knocked back a glass of lemonade as Bernie knocked back his can of soda.

"Congratulations once again and I hope that you both enjoy your new home and my famous lemonade as well," Bernie said.

"Thank you so much Bernie for all your help and the lemonade was fantastic, the best I ever had in years" I replied.

"You don't have to butter me up Olivia, it's good but not that good" as he laughed.

"No, I'm serious it's very good what is your secret?" I asked.

"If I told you that then I would have to…" as he paused.

"Kill me?" I asked.

"No, I was actually going to say hire you" As we both laughed. Bernie passed me another business card.

"Ok well off I go, if you have any questions don't feel free to call me" He was laughing.

"Well that was a joke, don't hesitate to call me and it was a pleasure meeting you both and doing business with you both" Bernie said.

"Well listen, I don't know if this is weird or not but my boyfriend and I are throwing a housewarming party a little get together. If you like to stop by, Craig and the guys will be here. I don't know if you do those types of things?"

"What partying? I don't always work you know" Laughing.

"Well if you play football I'm sure they will be playing." I replied.

"Oh no, but keep in touch I might be able to stop by but if not thank you for the invite. Anyways thank you that was nice of you." Bernie said.

"No problem, you're welcome." And that was that we locked up and Bernie went his way and I went mine.

Life was good for me, almost perfect. I had a home, a car, a career, a man I was very much in love with, but after that incident I was really never the same I kept trying to tell myself that it was a dream, a bad nightmare, but that wasn't true because like he said I never saw Bernie again after that. It had been five months and not a word from him at all for five months. All I did was try to figure out how he did what he did. Where was I at? I kept hearing his voice in my head saying,

"Olivia you are home silly" but was I really?

I have searched this entire home and found nothing what so ever he had to have been bullshitting me I would say to myself. I kept my promise and never moved or never told a soul about what had happened to me that day not Craig, not anyone. I mean gosh Craig was so happy our team was doing great and he was the star and as for myself well I was just happy that he was happy. My life was very simple, very boring, school, home, school, home, no hanging out just studying. I became obsessed with putting the pieces together about this man Bernie. I had to be careful though because the more I dug the more I could chance bringing him back out of his cage again and I was terrified of that.

I began looking into Master Reality off of his business card which now all of a sudden the number had been disconnected and also the name "Bernie" Burke Walters was that even his real name? I had to figure all of this out and yet after five months, I found nothing because it was all bullshit, all lies. I said to myself what do I do next? Because I will not allow this monster to get away with this. It wasn't until exactly five months and two weeks later that I went to campus and I saw everyone walking around whispering as if there were a secret party or something big going down. I paid no attention to it and went about my business.

When I got to class, Professor Lawrence who was my favorite Professor announced to the class that a 911 campus security call was made late last night that Maria Cooper was missing. The entire class was shocked by the devastating news it sent shock waves throughout the entire campus. Maria Cooper was a very nice girl and wouldn't hurt a fly. Who would do such a thing I said to myself? Professor Lawrence said that her boyfriend Clarence reported her missing after he came home from football practice and she wasn't home no call, no text, no note, no nothing. He called her parents to ask if they had heard from her but they hadn't either plus her phone would ring once and go straight to voicemail. Professor Lawrence said that campus security is working with the Los Angeles Police Department on all and any leads to find the where a bouts of Maria Cooper so if anybody knows anything that may be useful in finding her you are asked to contact the lead Detective working this case. As after 48 hours, she is an active missing case you are asked to contact Detective Ross, I believe it is Detective Eric Ross. Nobody could believe what had happened, but I knew who was behind this. It had to be him, I said to myself. A missing girl is his MO but I also said to myself that he will let her go if she cooperates, he let me go right? But what if it's not him? What if it is and he doesn't let her go? So many thoughts were running through my mind that I had to find out more about this case. Later on that day after class, a few of my girlfriends asked me if I wanted to go out for a few drinks to discuss Maria Cooper and what not so I did, we all went out for drinks at Applebee's to talk about it.

"So apparently Clarence and Maria got a place off of campus and when Clarence came home from football practice and drinks with his friends, Maria wasn't home and that wasn't like her," said one of the girls.

"Oh my god really? Do you know who they purchased the place from? I asked.

"Olivia this isn't about the place this is about Maria," Girlfriend replied.

"I know, just... Oh never mind." I replied.

"She probably isn't even missing, maybe she is cheating on Clarence and will pop up tomorrow or something like that," Other girl says.

"Ok so after Clarence left football practice where did he go? I asked.

"And when was the last time that he heard from Maria?" I continued.

"He left to Stoker's with a few teammates to drink beers but he told police that he spoke to her before practice which was around 5:30 pm." Girlfriend #1 replied.

"Ok and what time did he get home at?"

"I think he told police around 10:30 pm and waited up all night for Maria calling and texting her even reaching out to her parents who hadn't heard from her since 3:00 pm that afternoon," Girlfriend #2 replied.

"Where does Maria's parents live at?

"I don't know I think out of state though," Girlfriend #2 replied.

"Is it possible that she is headed to them maybe as a surprise?"

"Why would she do that and not tell Clarence?" Girlfriend #1 asked.

"Were they arguing at all? Did they get into a fight or argument or something?

"Not that I know of, I know they were happy about their new place they just moved into it about a week before you and Craig found yours," Girlfriend #2 replied.

She continued, "Olivia you should speak to Craig. He and Clarence are real cool as far as I know I mean they play for the same team and all.

"Yeah I will have to do that," I continued,

"Hey where is there house at? I would like to drop by and see how Clarence is doing."

"Um it's right off of campus but Clarence I don't think is staying there it's kind of like a crime sense now I think," Girlfriend #1 replied.

"Oh my god, is Clarence a suspect? I asked.

"I don't even know yet, that is a good question." Girlfriend #1 continued,

"I do remember Maria saying that the realtor was a nice guy who sold them the place though I remember that."

My heart almost sunk into my lap and I asked,

"Did she ever tell you his name?"

"Who the realtors name?" Girlfriend #1 asked.

"Yes, did she ever tell you his name?" I replied.

"Oh no she didn't, why do you ask that?

"Oh nothing, no reason at all I was just curious that's all." I continued,

"Hey, will you both excuse me for a minute? I'm going to step outside for a minute to check in with Craig."

"Ok girl, tell Craig we said hello with his fine ass," Girlfriend #1 said laughing.

"Yeah ok girl don't catch a beat down laughing back." I replied.

When I went outside, I called Craig. When he picked up, "Olivia where are you?" he asked.

"Did you hear about Maria? Are you ok?"

"Yes, I'm ok babe I am out with the girls at Applebee's having a drink." I replied.

"Yes I heard we are talking about it as we speak that is terrible news. How is Clarence holding up? Is he ok?"

"He is devastated you sure as hell picked a shitty day to decide to go out Olivia don't you think?" Craig asked.

"I know I'm sorry babe but I'm on my way home where are you?"

"On my way home now too, I will meet you there ok?" Craig replied.

"Ok baby, see you there in ten."

"Ok Olivia, no detours come straight home ok? Craig replied.

"No detours, straight home I love you see you soon."

"I love you too," Craig replied. Hurry up and then we hung up the phone. I went back into Applebee's to let the girls know that I was leaving,

"Oh no you have to leave now girl? They asked.

"Yes, my man wants me home I have to go." I replied.

"Man Olivia Craig has you whipped," Girlfriend #1 said as she began to laugh.

"Girl leave her alone," Girlfriend #2 said as she also began laughing.

"No, he doesn't I just respect my boo that's all" I replied laughing. "Bye girls, don't drink too much and be safe ok call me when you both get back home."

Craig was already there waiting for me by the time I got home in a panic I could tell that he wasn't happy with me going out on such a night but I needed answers and clues for which I couldn't tell him about. When I walked in, Craig said to me,

"So what do you think happened?"

"I don't know Craig, have you spoke to Clarence about it yet?" I asked.

"Yeah, a little I called him as soon as I heard about it he told me that this wasn't like her to just up and disappear like this that in his heart he knows there is something wrong." Craig replied.

"How did you first hear about this?" I asked.

"Well Coach Davis told us that Clarence told Professor Lucas about it and that Professor Lucas told Clarence to tell campus security about it."

"Who is Professor Lucas?"

"You know Professor Lucas is that theater Professor the drama class guy I don't have any classes with him." Craig replied.

"Neither do I, but I wonder why Clarence told him first?" I asked curiously.

"I don't know, maybe that is his favorite teacher I don't know, why? does that matter? Craig replied

"I don't know, maybe it doesn't." I said.

"Look Olivia straight home from class now ok last thing I need is for you not to go missing, you are my world other than football," he said of course laughing.

"Yeah, yeah, yeah, listen I'm going to clean up and start dinner are you hungry? I replied.

"No babe, I already eat I'm tired. I am just going to shower and go to bed is that cool? Craig replied.

"Yeah babe that's cool, I'm just going to study for a few I will meet you in there ok?

"Sounds like a plan babe see you in a few."

Craig went to shower and I sat on the couch just thinking no studying at all for me. I was too concerned with this Maria situation so I just sat there almost putting pieces together from a puzzle that I didn't have, I said to myself this has to be Bernie, it just had to be. So I got up walked over to the bathroom and asked Craig,

"Hey babe, where does Maria and Clarence live at?"

"Off of campus babe on the circle, Craig replied.

"Ok I will find it." I replied.

"What do you mean you will find it? Olivia let the police do their job, you are not a cop."

"Don't you find any of this to be a little strange? like Maria just up and leaving without a trace and all?" I asked.

"Very, but that is for the police to figure out and deal with not you Olivia," Craig replied.

"Ok Craig, but I was told if I can help in any way to do so," I replied.

"Yeah Olivia, with any information you can give you only know what the rest of us at school know so how can you possibly be of any kind of help?"

"Ok whatever Craig, sorry to bother you sorry that I even asked," I replied.

"Don't be like that Olivia, God bless your heart you are the sweetest person I know and I know you just want to help but you have to understand this is not your problem ok? Craig said.

"But isn't Clarence your friend?" I asked.

"He is a teammate, I don't know if I would say that he is my friend but he is a nice guy and all. Listen so what Olivia stay away from their house you're a nurse not a detective leave it alone either. Maria will turn up or let the police find a suspect either way its none of your business ok babe promise me that you will stay away from there house?" Craig said.

I took a deep breath and I said,

"Ok fine Craig, I will stay away from the house you happy now?" Craig yelling from behind the shower curtain yelled,

"Yes I'm very happy now, let's get to bed babe or at least I am. I have a very long day ahead of me tomorrow."

"Ok well you get some rest I have studying to do ok?" I said.

"Ok babe."

So I went back to the couch and began to say to myself tomorrow I am going to speak to as many people as I can about Maria and find out as much as I can because I believe that I can help the police find out what happened. I just can't let Craig know what I am doing so I ended up just passing out on the couch after taking my shower. It wasn't until morning time around 8:00 am that Craig came into the living room and woke me up with a cup of coffee.

"Rise and shine Olivia, you must have been studying hard you never made it to the bedroom last night." He said.

"Yeah I'm sorry babe, I had a lot of catching up to do I'm so sorry."

"Don't worry about it, you can make it up to me tonight," laughing Craig said.

"Yeah, I bet I can," as he gave me a kiss running out the door.

"Where you going," I asked him.

"Class babe where you should be going."

"Oh I'm sorry, I need to drink my coffee and wake up I'll see you later babe."

"Can't wait oh by the way practice at 6:00 pm tonight ok?" Craig asked.

"Got it, talk to you at 5:30 pm babe love you."

"I love you too babe."

That morning when I left the house, I said to myself, I can't leave it alone so I drove passed Maria and Clarence's place I just couldn't bring myself to stop because I kept hearing Craig's voice in my head saying Olivia stay away it's not your problem let the cops do their job and all that. But then the other half of me was saying what if I could help them with clues and what not? Maybe they over or under looked something that I can help them with? but instead I listened to Craig and just kept going past to school.

When I got to school, it was like the only thing that I could think about was what happened to Maria. So I decided to do something I knew would piss off Craig. I went to go speak to Coach Davis. I figured if Clarence told a Professor and it got back to Coach Davis who told Craig I guess I would start with the Coach first. So as I was looking for Coach Davis I passed a Professor Lucas's classroom so I said to myself this would be the better person to question first this is who

Clarence first spoke to about Maria missing and I wanted to find out why. I knocked on his door but nobody answered after about three knocks I grabbed the door knob and began to turn it as the door to Professor Lucas's classroom opened up. I poked my head around the corner and said,

"Professor Lucas, is anyone here?" I asked.

As I looked around and saw an empty classroom nobody was there as my voice echo.

"Professor Lucas, is anyone here?"

His classroom was like a theater so it was very big and very empty, so instead of just leaving, I decided to snoop around a bit looking for clues. I really had no idea what I was looking for, but I snooped anyways. I walked straight down the stairs to his desk and there were all sorts of papers on their absolutely nothing useful though just pretty much what his class was going over which was some sort of play. But then out of nowhere I hear,

"Can I help you young lady?" As I jumped, I said,

"I'm sorry, I didn't hear you come in, I'm sorry my name is Olivia you must be Professor Lucas?"

The man replied,

"No, I'm not actually, I am Professor Lucas' assistant.

"Assistant?" I continued,

"I don't get it, why would he have an assistant?" I asked.

"Well I'm more like his favorite student, I run the class for him when he is late, I grab his coffee, tea, things of that nature. My name is Dennis, May I ask Olivia what you are doing looking through the Professors paper work?"

"Oh I'm sorry, I was just being nosey please don't tell on me Dennis, but hey maybe you can help me since you are so tight with the Professor then?"

"Sure, what can I help you with Olivia?" Dennis asked.

"Well obviously, you know about Maria Cooper and Clarence right? Who doesn't? Anyways, I was wondering why Clarence came to Professor Lucas when he found out that Maria was missing? Why not go to the cops? Why not go straight to campus security? I figured well the only way to get that answer is to go straight to the source right?" I asked.

"Well that is a question really only Clarence could answer but I can tell you that Clarence is a good student that loves this course and looks as Professor Lucas as a mentor of some sort as do I, Professor Lucas is a very smart man. He is a master of his entire environment, he is in total control of everything around him and only a select few knows this Clarence and myself are one of those selective few." He said.

"Well he sounds like a very interesting man to say the least I would love to meet him and pick his brain but perhaps I should be speaking to Clarence then correct?"

"Yes, I'd say he would know more but the Professor will be in later should I tell him that you stopped by?" Dennis replied.

"No that is ok, I know that he is a very busy man I will catch him another time but thank you for your help and time I appreciate it," I replied.

"You are very welcome Olivia, oh and future reference don't snoop through the Professors stuff again next time. I won't be so nice and I will report you ok?" Dennis said.

"Well noted, thanks again," I said and we both walked out of Professor Lucas classroom.

Next person I needed to speak to was Clarence and find out why he told Professor Lucas before anyone else that Maria was missing. I was lucky enough to run into Clarence in passing later on that day and I asked him if he and I could speak after class and he agreed. He told me to meet him in the cafeteria and I remember seeing the look on his face as he sat in a quiet corner of the cafeteria looking so lost and hopeless. Everyone didn't know what to think about him or this entire situation with Maria, is he involved? What happened? When I sat down the first thing Clarence said,

"Look Olivia, I love Maria and I would never in a million years do anything to hurt her."

"I know that Clarence I'm not here about you, I'm just concerned like why did you tell Professor Lucas about Maria not coming home or calling, texting, all that first before telling security or police? Why tell him?"

"Honestly, because I was scared and he is like the only person that I can really talk to," Clarence replied.

"Why is that? More than your friends, more than your parents? I'm confused?" I replied.

"All my parents care about is football as do my friends, I'm not just a jock you know? My parents don't even know I'm taking theater as a course, my dad would laugh at me and call me a pussy and my mother would stand by him and my friends would agree as well," Clarence continued.

"You see, Professor Lucas understands me and thinks I have potential he is real cool we talk a lot he even passes me from time to time."

"What do you mean by that?" I asked.

"Sometimes, when I'm not passing in his class he would pass me you know." Clarence replied.

"Oh I see, so he told you to call the police when you told him about Maria?"

"No he told me to tell the campus security and they involved the police and now it's a missing person case."

"Ok so you had spoken to Detective Ross right?" I asked.

"Yes Olivia, why are you asking me all of this for?"

"Honestly Clarence, I don't know, I guess I want to help in any way that I possibly can, I'm worried for the both of you," I said.

"Well thank you Olivia but I'm going to go now I guess this is in god's hands now I hope this Detective finds out what happened to her."

"You two weren't fighting or anything like that at all?" I asked.

"Of course not, we were very much in love and still are and know there isn't anybody else as the cops have already asked me that question as well."

"Ok Clarence I'm sorry to bother you and I hope everything works out I really do."

"Me too Olivia me too."

Later on that day after school, I decided to drive passed Maria and Clarence place again. I wanted to go look for any clues that I could find so this time I stopped and got out of my car and began to look around the outside of the house. This had to be around 5:00 maybe later it was sunset so I could barely see anything but yet again as I went around to the back of the house I heard a voice yell,

"Freeze, stay where you are and put your hands up." As I jumped and yelled,

"I'm a friend of Clarence and Maria's."

"Ok stay still," as he cuffed me roughly and said turn around,

"Who are you? and what are you doing snooping around this house?" The man asked.

"Officer my name is Olivia Mathis, I'm a student at UCLA medical. I am a friend of Maria's and Clarence I was just wondering if he was home that's all."

"Let me see some ID ma'am? As he continued to say,

"I'm going to un-cuff you ok, I want you to slowly remove all items from your pockets slowly."

As he un-cuffed me, I began to panic, as I said

"I have nothing in my pockets officer other than my ID," as I handed it over to him.

"Ok stay still and calm until back up gets here ok?" He replied.

"Ok but officer is back up really necessary? I can just leave?" I asked.

"Yes it is and you can't leave until I find out why you are here."

"I just told you why I am here officer."

"Yeah ok, why didn't you just call him first to see if he was here?" "Is coming over to a friend's house unannounced, a crime sir?"

"Do me a favor and keep quiet until he gets here."

"Ok officer whatever you say."

"Thank you very much." He replied.

After about five minutes of standing, there a Detective came around back to the house and introduced himself to me as Detective Eric Ross and then said as the officer handed him my ID. "Miss. Olivia Mathis, may I ask what you are doing here?"

"Sir I am a friend of Maria and Clarence I heard what was going on with Maria so I came by to check on him and see how he was holding up that's all," I replied.

"Ok Olivia, this is now considered a crime scene and Clarence isn't staying here right now so when is the last time that you spoke to him?" Detective Ross asked.

"I would think that if he was your friend, you would have known that?"

"Well I haven't spoken to him since before Maria had gone missing this is why I came to see him it's been awhile." I answered.

"Ok Miss. Mathis you can go now, this is my card feel free to call me if you hear anything useful that can help us find Maria."

He continued, "Also call Clarence, he will tell you where he is staying at but stay away from this house it's an official crime scene now ok?"

"Ok Detective Ross, but what crime was committed here?"

"Bye Miss. Mathis, we will handle it, have a nice night." Detective Ross replied.

"Ok thank you officer or I'm sorry Detective oh and Detective umm…"

"Yes?"

"Never mind goodnight." I said.

"Be safe." And I left.

When I got home, my boyfriend Craig had already spoke to Clarence about our little conversation and he was very upset with me over it. I remember him yelling at me over the phone telling me,

"Didn't I tell you to stay out of their business?" I replied

"I know Craig, I know, but you don't get it, you don't understand," I replied.

"No Olivia, you don't seem to understand that this has absolutely nothing to do with you. Why would you go to Clarence and talk to him? What did you think that I wouldn't find out or something?"

"No Craig, I know you would but listen, I know I can help them and I need you for once to just trust me on this one please." I continued,

"I know what I am doing. There are certain things that I wish I could talk to you about and I promise when the time is right I will."

"Olivia what are you talking about?"

"Never mind Craig just understand that this is something that I have to do," I replied.

"Look Olivia, I'd tell you to stay home but I know that you're not so all I can say is be safe and we will talk more after practice ok?" Craig said.

"Ok Craig I love you."

"I love you too Olivia, talk to you later be careful." Craig replied.

"I will," and we hung up.

I knew what I wanted to do and that was to go back to Clarence house to look for some clues but what clues were I even looking for? I didn't know but yet again I went anyways but this time it was later in the day and I parked down the street that way no cops or security would see a car parked outside of the house. When I got to the house I looked all around it the front, and back yard, the sides, looked through windows, but found nothing. I knew what I needed to do next but couldn't bring myself to do it plus I was nervous to do it and that would be committing a crime by breaking out a window. I needed to look inside to see what I could find so I tried to open windows hoping that no neighbors would see or hear me but I couldn't get any open. After a while I got nervous and just left I was so disappointed that I didn't find anything that I started doubting myself like maybe Craig is right? Maybe I'm getting ahead of myself? Anyways I went back home and just waited on Craig to get home. I just kept thinking to myself what I went through was horrible and what if Bernie had Maria trapped somewhere doing the same thing to her? I know what that feels like and nobody should have to experience that nobody.

By the time Craig got home, he let me hear,

"Olivia what is going on? We really need to talk."

"What did I do now?" I asked.

"Don't give me that Olivia, now I have to go to practice and hear from guys on the team that my girlfriend was caught by the police snooping around Clarence and Maria's house? What is really going on Olivia? Is there something that you're not telling me?"

"No Craig I'm just trying to help."

"Stop Olivia, what did you mean by when you said you there were things that you wanted to tell me and you would when the time is right?"

"Exactly that Craig, look I love you, I really do but you're just going to have to trust me right now that's all I can tell you," I said. "Olivia, are you involved in this in any way shape or form? Craig asked.

"Of course not babe."

"Well if you know anything Olivia, you need to tell the police or campus security ok?"

"Of course, If I knew anything I would."

"Ok I'm going to jump into the shower oh and why did you go to Clarence house after I specifically told you not to?" Craig asked.

"I know, I'm sorry I shouldn't have baby I'm sorry," I replied.

"I don't know why you insist on learning the hard way Olivia? What do you want to go to jail or something?"

"Of course not, I'm sorry it was a bad idea, it won't happen again."

"Ok I'm jumping in the shower come lay down with me and watch some television ok?

"Ok sounds like a plan. I'll start dinner while you shower it's late I'm sorry."

Ok babe love you."

"I love you too."

After Craig got out the shower, he came out to dinner which was white rice and pork chops his favorite. We sat down in the living room instead and put on the television as we flipped through the channels we stopped on the news because we heard a reporter mention UCLA as we both jumped. The reporter goes on to say tragedy strikes UCLA campus students again as yet another girl goes missing. After the disappearance of Maria Cooper just over now three days ago a 911 call comes in just last night of yet another suspected missing woman. When Anthony Johnson told authorities that his girlfriend, Angel Clause hasn't been home since yesterday morning the Los Angeles police department had this to say.

"Good evening, this is Detective Eric Ross of the Los Angeles police department. We are actively following all leads in the disappearance of Maria Cooper as well as Angel Clause anyone who has any information about the two missing woman are advised to contact the Los Angeles police department immediately that's all, Thank you.

"Oh my god, what is going on?" I said to myself.

"Man Olivia this is getting serious Anthony. He also plays with me on the team, Craig said.

"Isn't Ange a cheerleader or something like that?"

"Yes she is, they both are really good people. Who the fuck is doing this? What the fuck is going on here?" Craig replied.

"I have no idea I'm shocked this is crazy,"

"Tomorrow at school is going to be crazy watch. I said I bet they still haven't found Maria and now Angel is missing there must be some kind of connection to all of this." I said.

"What do you mean? What kind of a connection?"

"Well, look Clarence and Anthony both play football and Maria and Angel were dating football players that's a strange connection don't you think?"

"I don't know what to think anymore Olivia." Craig replied.

"Hey, where does Anthony and Angel live at?" I asked.

"Oh no Olivia not this shit again?"

"I'm just wondering Craig, look remember you said yourself that Clarence and Maria had just got a new place off of campus like us right?"

"Yeah so what?" Craig replied.

"Ok, I'm going to find out where Angel and Anthony live maybe this is all connected."

"I don't know where they live babe again stay out of this please I'm begging you please for Christ sake, let the police deal with this."

"I will let them deal with it babe but you heard Detective Ross anything you know may help."

"But you don't know shit you're going to go to the police with that connection theory?"

"Yes why not it could help right? I asked.

"Oh my god, Olivia I'm going to bed take your shower and come do the same please."

"I will be right behind you babe but tomorrow, I'm going to see the Detective. I know I'm right that there is a strange connection going on here."

"Whatever you say Olivia good night."

"I'll be right there babe please don't be mad at me?"

I said to myself this is him it has to be everything in my gut tells me that I'm right I had this same feeling in my gut when he had me in his trap that's how I know that I am right. I said to myself I have to go see this Detective so I took my shower and I went to bed. But that next morning bright and early I left the house even before Craig got up because I couldn't sleep all I could only think about was where these poor girls were at. It must have been about 7 am Craig didn't leave for class until about 9 or 10 so I got dressed and jumped in my car and drove straight to the police station to see if I could speak to Detective Ross. When I got there I was told that Detective Ross wouldn't be in until around noon but that I could speak with another Detective or leave a message of any sort for Detective Ross. I declined and figured I just come back at noon or 1 pm to come speak to him face to face so I left back home to make Craig breakfast before he woke up. By the time Craig got up breakfast was ready and he never even knew that I had left for all he knew I got up early to make him a surprise breakfast. We spoke at the kitchen table for a few before he left for class about Maria and Angel that this was crazy and going to be nuts. He was worried about me how much I was invested into these disappearances but Craig just didn't know what I had been through and I couldn't tell him so I guess to him he thought that I was going crazy or something.

That afternoon I had to be to class at 11:00 am and I went but my mind was in the clouds I was looking at my professor but all I could see is his mouth moving but there were no words coming out of it. I kept imagining these woman screaming for help yelling for someone to help them much like what had happened to myself only much worse feeling hopeless just as I did. So I got up and walked straight out of class got into my car and drove to the other side of campus to the theater I figured I would catch Professor Lucas and speak to him about Clarence. When I got there I saw that his class was just getting out so as the students were walking out I was walking right in and down at the bottom of the class stood who I presumed to be Professor Lucas. I walked straight up to him and said,

"Hi my name is Olivia, I'm looking for a Professor Lucas. Do you know where I can find him at?

"Hi Olivia, I am Professor Lucas how can I help you?"

"Oh Hi, it is nice to finally meet you I was just wondering if I could speak to you a little about my friend Clarence?"

"I have a lot of students with that name but I am assuming that you are talking about Clarence Jones correct? Professor Lucas replied.

"Yes you assume correct."

"Ok sure what about Mr. Jones that you would like to know?"

"Well, you see everyone is saying that when Clarence girlfriend Maria went missing the first person he told was you. Not the police, not campus security, but you? So I'm just trying to get your point of view or rather your opinion as to why he would consult you before the authorities?"

"I see, well that is probably a question better fit for Mr. Jones to answer don't you think so?"

"You're right, that is why I have already spoke to him and your assistant student you have Dennis I believe his name was."

"Yes, Dennis is a good kid and much like Clarence they both I guess confide in me. I guess for guidance and what not." The Professor replied.

"Interesting why not go to the guidance counselor? You see? Why would he come to you sir?"

"I think because Clarence is ashamed of theater or what his teammates would think of him if they knew he was taking theater class so he speaks to me on a different level then others imagine what his teammates would think if they saw him weekly speaking to the guidance counselor?, I wish that I could be of more assistants to you Ms. Olivia, I'm sorry is there anything else that I can help you with? I am rather bust at the moment?

"No I guess, that is it Professor, thank you for your time you pretty much told me what they have already told me thank you."

"You are very welcome Olivia, have a nice day." The Professor replied.

"Same to you Professor."

As I left out of his classroom, I didn't know what it was but something rubbed me the wrong way about the Professor. I don't even know what it was, maybe because he seemed so nervous I don't know. Anyways, next stop was back to the police station to see Detective Ross so when I got back to the station I pulled up into the parking lot the same time as Detective Ross was he remembered me and said,

"Miss. Mathis what are you doing here?" I said

"Actually, I'm looking for you Detective do you have a minute?"

"Sure I do, follow me into my office."

As I followed him through the police station that place looked like a mad house, phones ringing, people yelling, it was like pandemonium in there. Once we got to his office he closed the door behind us and sat down as he offered me a seat as well. I told him that I wouldn't be long but asked him if they had any leads into both cases?

"You know I can't discuss an ongoing open investigation with you Miss. Mathis, but do you have any information for me?"

"Well I think I do, as a matter of fact."

"Well, do tell I am all ears?"

"I think there is a connection between the two woman."

"You do huh? How so? He replied.

"Well for one, they both attend UCLA and for two, they both are dating football players right?"

"Yes Olivia you are right."

I continued,

"So maybe it's someone very close to them that you guys are overlooking right?"

"Could be, but we are following all leads Miss. Mathis. Like I told you before, no arrest have been made but we are looking closely into everyone close to both women."

"Ok that is good, I felt so stupid Craig was right I had nothing, Ok Detective, I don't want to waste anymore of your time. I'm sorry to bother you." I said to him.

"You're not bothering me, you are concerned and I thank you for coming in and sharing that with me we are on top of this and whatever is going on we will get to the bottom of it I promise you that ok sweetie?

"Ok thank you, I know I'm not a cop and all but I do want to help in any way possible you know?"

"I understand and I thank you for coming in that is very brave of you. Are you friends with Maria and Angel?" Detective Ross asked.

"Not really friends, but acquaintances you know?"

"I get it, well thank you again and if you think of anything else feel free to call me you have my card right?"

"I do thank you." I said.

"Yeah it makes it easier than having to come out here just call me anytime or day with any information you come across ok?"

"I will, Detective thanks for seeing me."

"No problem. Have a nice day Miss. Mathis be safe out there," Detective Ross replied.

"You too." and I left.

As much as I didn't want to I know, what I needed to do was get into Clarence's place. I just had to. So after I left the police station, I headed towards Clarence place to search for some clues. I kept saying to myself there has to be something there that they didn't see or spot if there is I will find it I was just so nervous to break into his house I mean I want to help and all but at the same time I don't want to go to jail you know what I mean? Then I said to myself was it better to do it during the day or at night if I did do it at all? At night I wouldn't be able to see that well but during the day, everyone could see me so I had no idea what to do. Should I even do it at all? My mind was racing in twenty million different directions I just knew that I had to do something and think and do it fast. So I parked at a store nearby to stop and think what I should do or not do but my decision was to do it during the day so I just drove back to school to finish out my day but I told myself fuck it tomorrow night is the night I'm going to go inside and take a look around. In class I just day dreamed about it until Professor Lawrence noticed and called me out,

"Olivia am I boring you?"

"No sir I'm sorry, I didn't get much sleep last night I'm sorry."

"Perhaps then maybe you should go to bed earlier that way you wouldn't have to sleep or daydream during a lecture in my class?" "I'm sorry sir, it won't happen again."

"Let's hope not Miss. Mathis." Then Professor Lawrence went on to tell the class that another fellow student had gone missing.

"Well as you may or may not already know, but Angel Clause has now also gone missing." As the class began to speak to one another in total complete shock, Professor Lawrence said,

"Listen students, you all most stay safe and walk in groups if you all walk to campus this is something that is getting very serious and scary I want you all to be safe. If you see or hear anything about anything you are all urged to call campus security right away don't be a hero Maria Cooper and Angel Clause are both missing from this very campus."

"Have the police arrested anybody yet?" A student asked.

"To my knowledge, nobody has been yet but I'm not so sure. Anymore questions?"

"What about their boyfriends, are they suspects?" Another student asked.

"I am unsure I know about as much as you all know right now." As he continued,

"Ok anything else you are asked to contact the Detective handling both cases Detective Eric Ross of the Los Angeles Police Department. Class is dismissed see you all tomorrow be safe you all."

As I was leaving class, they announced the disappearance of now Angel Clause on the PA to the entire campus and now students were really freaking out and Detective Ross would have to give another press conference to assure students that a stop will be put to this mess because now students were really scared. With the disappearance of Maria students thought that maybe she left Clarence and would eventually show back up home. But now with Angel now missing it became very clear that we had a kidnapper on the loose and Detective Ross would now have his hands full. This went national it was all over television, radio, the internet, all in the papers, you name it and everyone especially women on campus were scared as hell and freaking out.

Later that day I went out and brought black gloves, a flashlight, and zip lock bags, for proof, evidence anything because tonight I will break into that house I said to myself. I have to help the police and these girls I owe it to them and myself I'm tired of being a victim and living in fear enough is enough tonight would be the night I would fight back. After school and after leaving the store I went back home and prepared myself mentally to do this I knew Craig would be at practice anyway. So my plan was to drive to the Clarence place park at a store nearby and walk over to it, now Craig's practice is usually from 5:00 pm and runs to 7:00 pm then he goes out with the guys for a drink or two till about 8:00 pm so he usually gets home at about 8:30 pm every night. This would give me 3 and a half hours to do what I needed to do and get back home before Craig did so now driving or walking nowadays in the mist of these disappearances wasn't easy anymore cops were everywhere on the lookout which made this even that much more difficult for me. So that night around 6:00 pm right after speaking with Craig and my parents I left and drove to a nearby corner store close to Clarence and Maria's house.

I parked and walked down to their house nervous as all hell trying to make sure that nobody was watching me and most of all that there were no cops around either. When I finally walked up to Clarence house, I went around the back to see if I could get in through a window of any kind but had no luck what so ever. So I picked up a rock and wrapped it in a cloth and broke out a piece of the window right above the door knob just enough so that I could open it. There was no alarm thank god but the shattering of the glass was enough noise to draw attention so by now you could imagine my heart is racing and I am nervous as hell I unlocked the door wearing gloves and proceeded to walk into the house. Right now I am in the kitchen and I'm looking in cabinets, on the kitchen table, the fridge, you name it looking for any kind of clues. Then I went to the living room looking in the couch and all over the dining room as well but found nothing then I went into the bathroom snooped through there and the guest bed room still coming up with absolutely nothing. Then I walked into Clarence and Maria's bedroom and snooped around in there for a few and after about five minutes of looking around I couldn't believe what I had spotted. Right there off on the side of the bed in between the bed and night stand was a pitcher of lemonade and a glass I was in total disbelief not just any lemonade it was in fact Bernie's lemonade. Remember the one he said he gives to all his buyers? The one he said he basically drugged me with? I was sick to my stomach I couldn't believe it but I knew I was right all along. This sick fuck Bernie was behind this and I knew it all along what the fuck I said to myself? So I grabbed the pitcher with some of the lemonade still in it and began to rush out for the back door in a panic.

As I was running for the back door I tripped and dropped the pitcher and glass on the carpet and spilled the lemonade as I said to myself "fuck" I dropped the damn evidence "oh my god" I am so fucking stupid. Well even if there is a little bit in it like a drop or so that can still be used right? The glass has to have finger prints on it right? I had to get this to Detective Ross right away I said to myself. I got up and went out the back door and headed back to my car and drove straight back home I must of got back just before Craig got back home because it felt like as soon as I undressed and hid the bag of stuff I found at Clarence house Craig was calling me to tell me that he was on his way home and felt like pizza tonight and that he was picking one up. I told him that was fine with me all I could think about was what to do now? Remember what Bernie told me? Not to tell anyone or he would come for both me and Craig. I kept saying to myself how is he getting these girls? And where are they now? I can't just continue to sit on what I knew right? I was so scared and confused on what to do next I just had to prove to myself that I was right and that this was Bernie and that he was back but now that I have opened Pandora's box I wish that I hadn't because by doing so I will have put my life and Craig's in jeopardy and he doesn't even know it. What should I do I kept asking myself? Even if I give this to Detective Ross to run prints he will wonder why I want it ran? And where I got it from? and assume I was the one who broke into Clarence place when they find out someone did which I knew would be soon.

By the time Craig walked in, he looked very tired and asked me how my day was? And if I had stayed out of trouble today.

"Yes babe of course, and my day has been hectic and long how about yours babe?"

"Same here, everybody is freaked out about these two missing girls I wish things could just go back to normal already. Let me ask you Olivia, who do you think is behind all of this mess? Do you think these girls are dead?"

"Yeah me too babe, but I have no idea and I hope they are alive. I mean this is scary do the cops know anything yet? How is Clarence and Anthony doing? I could only imagine how they must be feeling right now."

"I have no idea what the cops know and Clarence is playing ball keeping busy and Anthony hasn't been to school since Angel went missing." Craig continued,

"So I have no idea what's up with him but guys on the team said he is staying with family and is taking it very badly. Shit I would be too though if I were him Clarence still playing ball is kind of weird I wouldn't be but hey people grieve the way they grieve you know what I mean?"

"Yeah I know what you mean," then I said,

"Well look babe, I've had a long and stressful day I think I'm just going to take my shower and go to bed is that ok with you?"

"Sure babe, I am right behind you yeah today has been a stressful day I think for the entire school." As we both jumped into the shower then had an early night as we both went to bed together for the first time in what felt like a long time.

That next day in school, word already got out about someone breaking into Clarence and Maria's place and because I was spotted outside of it once before snooping Detective Ross asked to speak with me pulling me out of class for all to see. When we got to campus security offices, Detective Ross told me to have a seat.

"What is going on Detective?" I asked.

"Well Miss. Mathis, we meet yet again. Are you aware of that someone broke into Clarence Jones house the other day?" Detective Ross asked.

"Yes, umm I just heard about it, that is just terrible."

"Yes it is when did you hear about it?"

"Just a few minutes ago before you came to get me."

"So you wouldn't by any chance know of anyone who might have done or wanted to do anything like this right?"

"No sir why would I?"

"Well because I did catch you snooping around that house once before correct?"

"Snooping? No visiting or dropping by, Yes."

"Yes Miss. Mathis, we seem to both remember that incident differently nevertheless I need you to stay away from that house are we clear on that?" Detective Ross said.

"Yes sir crystal clear sir."

"Good. Now get back to class we are done here, thank you for your time." As I got up to leave Detective Ross continued on to say,

"Oh and by the way Miss. Mathis, I will be watching you take care of yourself."

"That is fine by me thank you and same to you." As I turned around and left the office. Instead of going back to class I left campus and went back home I needed to figure out what I was going to do with the pitcher of lemonade and glass. It wasn't like I could just hand it over to Detective Ross because now the guy was looking at me as a suspect mean while I'm trying to help him out. So I said to myself I'm just going to mail it to the police department I went out and bought a box, bubble wrap, and all, plus made sure even to leave a little note in it saying "Run me for finger prints" I said fuck it Bernie was going down I couldn't sit back and stay quiet any longer.

After I sent it in I just waited to see what would happen but another week had gone by and I heard nothing about anything no prints, no arrest made, no nothing, and these girls were still missing vanished without a trace. So I had to go see Detective Ross to pick his brain and find out what he knew or didn't know for that matter. I remember knocking on his door as he said,

"Miss. Mathis, come in and what do I owe the pleasure?"

"Sir I think I might have some useful information about Maria and Angel." I replied.

"Yeah like what?"

"Did you look into the connection theory that I told you about yet?"

"Umm yes actually Miss. Mathis I did."

"And?" I asked.

"We are looking into all leads Miss. Mathis, you also know that I can't be discussing and open and ongoing investigation with you as well." Detective Ross replied.

"Well why is this taking so long? These girls have been missing for a long time now sir?"

"These things take time Miss. Mathis, trust me, we will find whoever is responsible for this just leave it to us we are the police you are the student ok?"

"Is there any new information? Any new leads?"

"Miss. Mathis, you are very persistent aren't you? So I've heard."

Detective Ross continued,

"I will tell you one thing and then you need to leave ok?"

"Deal."

"Ok well about a week ago, a package was delivered from an unknown sender with no return address which I won't reveal. What was in the package but the note with the package asked us to run the items for prints." He said.

"Ok and what happened?"

"Absolutely nothing that's the thing, there were no prints on the items. None whatsoever, all wiped clean like it had just been purchased from the store."

"What? Really? Are you sure?" I asked in total disbelief.

"Yes really, you seemed very shocked Miss. Mathis why is that?"

"For the same reason you are sir that is crazy did you run it more than once?"

"Of course we did, in fact we did it three times just to make sure."

"Wow that's unbelievable, what do I have to do?" I continued,

"I mean, what do we have to do?"

"You mean what do I have to do? Why do I have a feeling that you're not telling me something Miss. Mathis? I gave you that information so now what do you have for me?"

"No I don't sir, just simply trying to help that's all."

"Go on Olivia, we will be in touch."

"Ok Detective, thanks for your time," and I left.

When I left the his office, I was in disbelief as I said to myself no prints? Are you kidding me? So my next move when I got home later that evening was to find the business card that Bernie had given to Craig and I when we first moved into the home. I said to myself I'm going to see what I can find out about this prick but why do I keep pursuing this guy? But it was because I had to, it was because there was nobody else that knew about this guy but me. I began to look all over the house for that card so much that Craig had asked me what I was looking for so disparately. I told him that I lost an important school paper that I was working on so that he wouldn't question me about the business card. The less that Craig knew the better and finally after about a half hour later of looking or so I found the business card that I had been looking for and it read "Master Realty Company" Realtor and President Burke Walters and the number to the real estate company and an address but no picture what so ever. Well my plan was tomorrow morning to find out where to point Detective Ross to? To basically point him in the direction of the real estate company because they can investigate that after I do some digging myself but I knew I had to tread softly and do things as quiet as possible.

So early that morning, I called the number on the front of the business card and after one ring the operator says, "The number that you are trying to reach has been disconnected." So what do I do now? No prints, no number. I said to myself if I can't find him, the police damn sure wont because I knew more than they did. The only thing left to go off of was the address on the front of the card which read "15161 West Sunset Blvd Los Angeles, CA." So as Craig was getting ready to leave for class, he asked me,

"Olivia listen, you didn't break into Clarence's place did you?"

"No why do you ask me that?"

"Well because the cops did find you over there once already so... Look Olivia, if you know anything about anything you know that you can talk to me right? I mean you know that I am here for you right or wrong I will always be here for you I hope you know that right?"

"Of course, I know that baby that's why I love you so much, go on and get to class I'm going to clean up before I leave I don't have class until 1 pm today babe."

"Ok babe, stay out of trouble today and I love you too be safe out today shit keeps getting crazier and crazier out here every day babe."

"I will babe, don't worry about me. I will be fine," then we gave each other a kiss and Craig walked out the front door.

Now my next move was to clean up the house and then leave out to find Master Realty Company because Sunset Blvd. was about a ten minute drive from campus. So after I was finished cleaning the house I left to go find this place and once my navigation system told me that I was at my destination I was in like a little old school strip mall. So I pulled up outside of the place and it looked abandoned, there was an empty parking lot, and businesses that were shut down and empty, there was dust all on the windows, it looked like there had been nothing in that place for years. I said to myself wow another dead end? Was this guy even a realtor? No prints on the cup or pitcher, a disconnected phone number, and now a false address? I had absolutely nothing to go on it was as if Bernie didn't exist I was so lost and confused as to what the fuck was going on? I had to speak to Clarence again to ask him a few more questions. So when I finally got to school I tracked him down yet again and asked him if we could talk just really fast? That I had to ask him just a few questions and he agreed.

"Come on Olivia, make this quick I have to go. You should be a cop not a nurse what's up?"

"Ok Clarence, you got a house around the same time that Craig and I did right off of campus right?" I asked.

"Yeah so what's your point?"

"Well what realty company did you go through to get it?"

"Umm, I don't really remember but dude gave me his card I know that."

"Great! I need you to find me that card ok? The realtor that sold you the home was his name by any chance Bernie?"

"Yeah, yeah, Bernie he was a real cool dude he was easy to work with real friendly guy he dropped us off a fruit basket and tea real nice guy."

"And your house is on the circle so is mine," Said to him and myself out loud.

"Yeah so what? Olivia what are you talking about?"

"Umm, nothing. Hey where can I find Anthony at?"

"I don't know, I haven't seen him in a while why?"

"I just need to speak to him. Also, hey do you know where he and Angel live at?" I asked.

"Yeah, they also stay on the circle why?"

"Are you kidding me? You're serious?"

"Yeah why?"

"I need to find out what realty company they went through fast."

"Why? Olivia you sound crazy right now what you think the realtor is behind all of this? Do you know how crazy that sounds Olivia?"

"Does it though? But what if I am right? Think about it Clarence, we all live on the circle and all bought from the same realty company I bet? Maria went missing right? So did Angel and I bet they went through the same company as well too?

"But Maria wasn't missing from the home she never came home."

"But how do you know that for sure? Maybe she got home before you then vanished before you got home? She didn't have a vehicle so you wouldn't know right?"

"But there was no break in though?"

"He is the realtor, he maybe has a spare key? or maybe she let him in? You never know Clarence think about it? I asked.

"Ok Olivia, I have go I'll look for that card tonight and what not but stop over thinking so much try to get more rest."

"Just find me that card please. Also hey do you by any chance have Anthony's phone number or anything?"

"No but I can get it for you though."

"Please do, that would be great."

"Ok aye, here is my number. By the way, shoot me yours through a text and I'll let you know when I find the card and get Anthony's number ok?"

"Ok great thanks so much Clarence, I really do appreciate it."

"No problem, be safe Olivia."

"Same to you," and we both went our separate ways.

So I finished the school day asking myself should I tell Clarence about what Bernie did to me? I knew that I was getting close but the closer that I got I would have to fill someone in on what I know and that was the hardest part about this all. Later on that night while just relaxing with Craig watching a movie, I got a text on my phone from Clarence telling me that he found the card and that he also got Anthony's phone number for me. I replied to the text saying "thank you very much" and that we will get to the bottom of this together. Clarence replied "let's see" then I had to hear it again from Craig as he asked,

"Who is that messaging you at this time of night Olivia?"

"A friend Craig and this time of night? Its 10:00 pm?" I replied.

"Well, tell your friend it's my time with my woman. Your friends have you all day."

"Yes daddy," as I laughed,

"Sorry baby."

"Yeah, yeah, yeah," as we both laughed at each other.

That next day, I called Anthony around 12:00 noon and to my surprise he answered right away and said,

"Hello?"

"Hi Anthony, this is Olivia Mathis you play football with my boyfriend Craig?"

"Yeah, hey what's going on? Who gave you my number?" He continued to say,

"I changed it, this is a fairly new number."

"I got it from Clarence, I'm sorry but I needed to speak to you it's urgent."

"Oh ok well what's up? What's going on?"

"Well, hey I know this is going to sound crazy but I think I might know who is responsible for the disappearance of both Angel and Maria."

"What? Who?"

I continued to say,

"Where do you and Angel live? Did you all get a house on the circle off of campus?"

"Yeah why do you ask?"

"Do you by any chance remember the realty company that you went through? Or the realtors name that sold you the home?"

"Hell yeah, not the company but I do remember the pricks name because that asshole rubbed me the wrong way from the start."

He continued, I always felt like he was hitting on Angel every time that he came around his name was Bernard or something like that." "Do you mean Bernie?" I asked.

"Yeah, yeah, that was his name why do you ask? Do you think it's him behind this shit?"

"Anthony, I'm sure do and I'm going to need your help to prove it ok?"

"Ok cool what do you need from me?"

"First, let's start with any paperwork you have to that house." I said.

"All I have is a business card and another piece of paper saying that I own the place and what not." Anthony replied.

"Ok well, can you get it all together and meet me at say the Starbucks on Sunset Blvd at 5:30 pm?"

"Yeah, I can do that. Don't stand me up though."

"No, I won't do that I'll be there, thank you so much see you then."

"Ok see you then."

Now I needed to text Clarence to let him know to bring the business card and to meet us also at the Starbucks on Sunset Blvd at 5:30 pm as well. After I had text him the information he told me that he didn't know if he could make it because of practice though. I told him to skip it that this was very important that I had very good news to tell him about my so called theory and to make sure that he was there.

That evening at 5:30, I was the one late and both Clarence and Anthony were both there waiting for me sitting down at an outside table.

"Here is the business card and paper I signed from the guy now what? Anthony said.

As I looked over the paper and card,

"This sun of a bitch"

"Here is the business card he gave us too so what's the deal Olivia?" Clarence asked after handing me the card.

"I have to go, I can't miss all of practice," Clarence continued.

"Ok so we all have the same business cards with the same realtor and same company, so I want you both to call the number on these cards from your phones then tell me what happens?"

As Clarence and Anthony both pick up their cell phones and dial the number on the card, ring, ring, ring, they both look up at each other after a second or two as I did as well, they both say out loud to one another the number is disconnected.

"Hmm isn't that ironic? I said and continued,

"I want you both to type in the address to Master Realty Company into your navigation systems on your phones then tell me what it says?"

As both Clarence and Anthony type in the address into their navigation system, it pulls up that their destination is located right across the street from the very Starbucks that they are sitting at. As they both look up and say,

"Olivia what's really going on here?"

"That's why I asked you both to meet me here at this specific location." I continued,

"What do you see across the street over there?"

"That don't look like no realty company that looks more like an abandoned strip mall, their isn't shit running over there not even a sign." Anthony replied.

"It looks like he just put some address on a business card with a fake number and all that. Hell, is Bernie even his real name?" Clarence said.

"This is what I've been trying to explain to you both. Nothing is adding up do you both believe me now? He is the only person with access to all of our homes and clearly he isn't who he says he is so the real question is who is this man? Also he didn't do any of this by using a key that I know for a fact because for starters, Maria as you said never came home right Clarence?" I asked.

"Yeah that's right." Clarence replied.

"But if my theory is correct she was home before you got home and he got her before you got there." I continued,

"Now Angel disappeared from the home no breaking or entering no nothing which would suggest she either let him in or he walked himself in. But using a key she either would have seen him or heard him come in unless she was sleeping or was in the shower right?"

"True, but you just said you know for a fact that he didn't use a key why did you say that Olivia?" Clarence replied.

"Let's go check out this strip mall real quick," as I completely ignored the question.

"Ok we can do that but answer my question first?" Clarence asked again.

"Ok well because he seems too smart to do something so dumb he would be seen it's too risky you know what I'm saying?"

Anthony didn't seem too convinced but went along with the idea anyways. As we all jumped into our cars and went across the street to look into the windows of this place you could clearly see that Clarence wanted to leave.

"There is absolutely nothing in this place. There is dust and webs everywhere he never used this place it's all a lie we need to go to the police with this, but look I have to get to practice I'm already late as it is.

"Olivia I got you what you needed, I believe you. Now let's get to the bottom of this, I want my girl back please." Anthony said.

"I will do my best I'm just glad that you finally believe me now." "I have to go, see you both later," Clarence said as he jumped in his car and left while Anthony and I stood there in total disbelief. "So what's next? We go to the police right?" Anthony asked.

"Well yes and no."

"What does that mean Olivia? I feel like there is something that you're not telling us. I don't know man."

"You're right and I promise you that when the time is right that I will, but all I can say for now is that I'm a victim too that is why I am so invested if that helps any."

"A victim? How Olivia? I need answers please?"

"Give me some time, I will explain but for right now we need to talk to Detective Ross about all this together are you willing to do that? Because I don't know if Clarence is?" I said.

"I have no problem with that, if it will bring me back my Angel or let me know what's going on at all, so please help me Olivia."

"Ok I will do my best we need to all talk to Detective Ross first so what you can do right now is work on convincing Clarence on helping us please."

"I got you, let's do this." Anthony replied.

Later that night when I got home, Craig got in a little after me and when I asked him how his day was he replied,

"Wow, Olivia I had an awesome night tonight babe the coach said that I am becoming one of the best quarterbacks that UCLA has ever seen in a long time. Babe I work so hard on that field and I finally feel like it's finally all paying off because coach has been riding me all year and never complimented me up until today it was crazy babe."

"Babe I am so proud of you that is great I told you to give it time and that it would all work out for you because you're the best boo," as we both laughed.

"Yeah well I guess I am the best huh babe?," Laughing.

"Yes you are the best because I'm not on that field if I were on there you wouldn't even be noticed," Laughing.

"I know that because everybody would want to tackle you but then I would have to kill them guys because you are mine," as Craig grabs me and lifts me up by my thighs and starts to kiss me.

"Yes babe I am all yours my big handsome football player you are," as we both continued to laugh at each other.

Craig took me into the bedroom as we made passionate love throughout the night. That next morning,

"You know what, I did find to be funny babe though the other day?"

"No babe what's that?"

"Coach chewed Clarence out for being late to practice and the funny thing about it is that, Clarence has never been late to a practice ever. He is a star linebacker so coach was a little upset. But given what he is going through with Maria, coach went I guess a little easy on him but you could tell he wasn't very happy and to all of us that was weird because Clarence never is late or misses a practice he usually is the first person there he is almost like a locker room leader you know? So that was strange you know what I mean?"

"Yeah that is but maybe something important came up you never know? Well the good thing is that he showed up at all right?" I said.

"Yeah I guess you are right, well I'm going to go to the gym and get an early workout in what are your plans for today babe other than class?"

"Um nothing really, might just hit up the mall later for some shoes but that's about it that I know of babe." I replied.

"Ok babe see you tonight be safe and try to stay out of trouble ok?"

"Of course I will babe, I'm headed to class too right behind you I will see you later boo."

"Ok cool."

We gave each other a kiss and went our separate ways. I text both Clarence and Anthony and asked them to meet me at the police station that all three of us needed to tell Detective Ross what we all know. So I went to class and just waited to hear back from the two of them throughout the day and the first person to respond was Clarence to my surprise and furthermore that he was with it and agreed with me that we should. I kept hitting up Anthony but to no avail he never wrote back or called back throughout the day until like ten minutes before I was about to meet up with Clarence he text me back and said that he needed more time to think about it. I replied ok but what is there to think about? We know it's him it all points to him and everything we know about him is a lie and fake? Anthony replied and that's what scares me about this all, we don't know shit about him and if we bring this to the police they will start looking at us as suspects you know? I tried to convince him that they already did and that we have enough proof for them to look into this all and finally find out what's going on. Now after messaging back and forth for about thirty minutes, I finally convinced Anthony to go along with it. Now the plan was for the three of us to go to Detective Ross office with our business cards and paperwork and explain to him what we believe is going on and I finally had both Clarence and Anthony on board. But being that Anthony was a little hesitant, it took a little longer than expected but once we all got together we all drove to the police station separately to speak to Detective Ross collectively.

Once we got there just with my luck the Detective wasn't, so we waited for about an hour before he finally showed up. He told us to follow him into his office while Clarence and I looked of confidence. Anthony looked scared straight, he was so nervous. He was nervous because he got it the worst by the media because he left school after Angel disappeared plus she disappeared right from the home unlike Maria who allegedly never came home. Now before I tell you what took place in Detective Ross's office I need to further explain to you all how both woman went missing in further detail.

Now it was said that while Clarence came home after football practice and a night with teammates as he always did his girlfriend of three years never showed up home. She usually was always home granted that they just had recently moved into this new home in the last two weeks she would always be home before Clarence to prepare him dinner much like I do for Craig. Now Angel on the other hand disappeared from within the home which was the crazier one of the two disappearances because Anthony claims he was at practice but had spoken to Angel before and throughout practice and that she was home the entire time so what makes him believe that she was taken from the home? He would explain this in full detail in Detective Ross's office as the three of us walk into the Detectives office I can remember the look he had on his face seeing all three of us together he was very confused at this point or so I thought he was.

"Wow," The first thing he said.

"Have a seat you all, now tell me what's up? This is definitely a surprise to say the least. What's the deal? I'm glad to see you back Anthony."

I did most of all the talking as I usually did.

"Well Detective I think the three of us agree on to who we believe is behind this all and who you should be looking into not that I'm trying to tell you how to do your job or anything like I said before just trying to help you know what I mean?" I started.

"Yes of course, I'd hope that you wouldn't be trying to tell me how to do my job, so with that being said what do you have for me Miss. Mathis?" Detective Ross asked.

"Well, I know this is going to sound a bit crazy but just hear me out please." I continued to say,

"So as you know already Clarence, myself and Anthony, we all live off campus on the circle and all bought homes around the same general time so I asked myself who would have access to these homes? And as crazy as it may sound I said to myself well let me find out what realty company did Clarence and Anthony go through? And I came to find out that it's the same one that I went through but that's not all, here is the weird part. So I call the realty company that is on the business card and paperwork of purchase of the home the deed you know? And guess what?"

"What?" Detective Ross asked.

"The number is disconnected, but wait it gets even weirder. I go to the address on the business card and paperwork and guess what?"

"What?" Detective Ross asked again.

"It takes you to an abandoned strip mall, this is crazy plus the realtor is the same guy who sold to all of us. This has to be the guy right Detective?"

"Really interesting, do you have the business cards and paperwork here with you?"

"Yes we do Detective."

"Great, I'm going to need to make a copy of all that now." We all replied,

"Ok," and handed it all over to Detective Ross as he said,

"Give me a minute while I go copy all of this hang tight."

"Ok cool," The three of us replied.

Once he came back in, he gave us back our original copies.

"Ok thank you all, that is very, very, very, good work I will definitely be looking into this Burke Walters guy at Master Realty."

"Very good work? That's it? Why don't you go arrest this fucking guy?" I asked pissed off.

"That's not how this works Miss. Mathis. Just because you come into my office with this information you have, I can't just go arrest someone." He continued,

"Now this is proof of some snake shit going on but not proof that he kidnapped some college woman you understand? Now calm down and don't ever cuss at me again are we clear?"

"Clarence and Anthony, my silent partners do you want to say anything?"

Anthony gets up and walks out of the office.

"Oh that's great, your girlfriend disappears you walk out that's good stuff what a good guy you are." I said.

"Olivia leave him alone and just let the Detective handle this please." Clarence said to me.

"What is this? Am I the only one who gives a damn about these woman?"

"Miss. Mathis that is enough calm yourself down now, maybe you should listen to your friend Clarence and let me do my job." As Detective Ross yelled.

"Yeah because you're doing such a bang up job as it is" I replied underneath my breath.

"That will be all Miss. Mathis, I thank you for your help but you are not a cop, I am. Now I have already told you that I will look into this all as soon as possible ok?"

"Ok but how? it's a false number and address?" I asked.

"They always slip up, so once again let me do my job. Thank you that will be enough." Detective Ross replied.

As Clarence and I both got up and began to walk out the office, I look over at him.

"What was that?" I continued as we were now outside of the office.

"I mean you and Anthony not saying a word in there, it's almost as if I lost these woman not you all thanks for having my back." "Olivia what the fuck are you so invested in this for anyways huh? I mean what do you want from us? We are going through enough we came up here with you didn't we? We met up with you at Starbucks didn't we? We gave you all the information you asked us for didn't we? I think the bigger question is how or why are you tied up in all of this? What is the real reason you care so fucking much and stop saying it's because you want to help. Olivia everyone is tired of hearing it even from the looks of it so is the Detective." Clarence said.

"You know what Clarence, fuck you I don't need this shit I'm out of here." I replied.

"See, you can't even be honest with yourself Olivia. Good see you around."

As we both went our separate ways. I couldn't help but feel as if I were the only person who cared about what's going on with these woman I mean are they dead? And they alive? Are they being tortured like I was? We need to know ok maybe Clarence had a point maybe. I only care for my own reason but by helping them, I help myself because I was in their shoes at one point. But who could I really tell this to? Who would even believe me?

That night, I just was at home preparing dinner. I had text both Clarence and Anthony to apologize for the way I acted but neither of them responded to my messages. I felt so bad and lost I really just wanted to help not only them but myself as well and now I messed everything up. Once Craig got in from football practice he came in all happy and gave me a big hug and kiss I hadn't seen him this happy after a practice in a while he smelled of sweat and beer.

"Hey babe you must have had a good time tonight?"

"Yeah I did babe. Today at practice, coach said that he has never seen a player work as hard as I do and praised me in front of the entire team it was great!"

"That's awesome babe, I am so proud of you I really am."

"Thanks babe but what's wrong with you? How was your day?"

"Not so good but I don't want to ruin yours or rain on your parade tell me all about your day babe."

"No babe that's ok will talk about mine after, babe what's wrong? Are you ok?"

"Yeah I'm ok, I just had a rough day that's all no big deal babe, but it looks like you had fun tonight I can smell it all over you?"

"Yeah it's been one hell of a day you will never guess who I ran into today babe."

"Who is that?"

"Oh before I forget here is your coffee and creamer, I ran into that guy Bernie who sold us this place the realtor."

I dropped the glass that I was holding in total disbelief of what I just heard and spit out my drink and began choking.

"What did you just say?" Craig rushed over to me.

"Damn it babe are you ok? What's wrong? You look like you just saw a ghost or something? You sure you're alright?"

"No I'm ok," while I reached down to clean up the mess that I just had made with the glass of juice that I was just holding. I continued,

"Did he say anything to you at all? I asked.

"Yeah we spoke for a few then he came out to drink with me and the guys, hell he even paid for all the drinks we had."

"Are you serious?" I continued,

"Craig what did he all speak to you about this is very important?"

"I don't know, just about this place, school, football, bullshit why is it important?"

"That's it? Was that all he spoke to you about?"

"Yeah what's up with all the questions? Oh and he asked about Clarence and Anthony how they were doing and what not. He was talking about how messed up of a situation this is and how this is a good peaceful area and what not, he is a cool guy I had a lot of fun."

"Did he give you a number or anything? Like anyway to get in touch with him again?"

"Wait, wait, wait. What is the deal Olivia? Why all the questions though?" I was getting loud,

"Just answer the god damn question please?"

Craig was shocked

"No he didn't give me a number any of that. We have it already, why do you need it anyways Olivia?"

"Oh god never mind, listen to me very carefully babe. If you ever valued anything I ever said before, value this and please if you see him again stay away from him and tomorrow we need to change the locks on all these doors."

"Ok Olivia and now you can tell me what for?... Wait what do you actually think our realtor is the kidnapper?" He was laughing.

"You know what, your drunk and right now you are being a complete asshole so guess who can sleep on the couch tonight? I'm going to bed, serve yourself dinner you jerk, good night!" As I walked past him towards our bedroom went into it slammed the door shut and locked it behind me.

"Come on Olivia open the door please don't be like that your tripping, I'm tripping, it's been a long day baby just open the door and let's talk ok? Please babe I'm sorry I was just playing ok?"

I opened the door real fast and threw him a pillow and blanket out the door with a fresh pair of clothes then slammed the door back in his face.

"Babe please don't be like this"

After about another ten minutes of begging, Craig finally left me alone took his shower and went to bed. He pisses me off when he drinks too much but the nerve of this guy Bernie right? I was terrified he come back and I knew that it was my fault and that something bad was about to happen. I felt it in the pit of my stomach I was scared very scared and had absolutely no idea what to do or who to speak to. Craig won't believe me even if I told him so who should I tell this to? Because the cat was out of the bag. Bernie must live locally I said to myself is he watching us? This is scary, so after completely freaking myself out for an hour or so I took my ass out to the living room and cuddle up with Craig on the couch. It was safe to say that Craig that next morning didn't really remember much of our conversation the night before and I guess that was beneficial for me because I wasn't ready to tell him about Bernie yet or even at all for that matter. So that morning Craig just simply told me that he was sorry for whatever he said or did wrong the night before and we kissed and made up I left it at that made him breakfast as we both got ready for our day. I made the conscious decision to share that awful time that happened with Bernie to Clarence and I don't know why he first out of everybody but it just seemed right and he was the easiest to talk to or maybe to convince or maybe it was simply because he was the first victim in all this outside of myself. So that morning after Craig left for class I messaged Clarence and told him that we needed to talk that

I was ready to tell him why I was so invested in helping out. I told him that I would meet him at that same Starbucks again on Sunset at noon to meet me there and to my surprise he agreed. Later that afternoon around 12:30 or so I reached the Starbucks and Clarence was already there patiently waiting. As he sat there with two coffee on the table one for me and one for himself,

"Ok Olivia what's up? Talk to me?" asked Clarence.

As I exhaled loudly,

"Look this is very difficult to talk about and you are actually the first person that I've ever told this to ok. Not my parents, Craig, the police, nobody, what I'm about to tell you can get a lot of people hurt even killed Clarence I need you to understand that are we clear?"

"Well damn, I don't even know if I even want to know now damn Olivia what are you involved with?"

"Well you either want to know or you don't Clarence you kept pushing to know why I cared so much right? Well now is your chance to know but it's now or never so it's your call." As he sits there thinking to himself,

"What do you mean by telling me people can get hurt or killed? What do you mean by that?"

"Exactly what I said by me telling you what you want to know I will be putting mine, yours, Craig's, everybody's life in danger so do you still want the truth? Be careful what you wish for? I tell you what I am going to the bathroom Clarence think about it some more real quick and have an answer for me by the time that I get back deal?"

"Umm ok I guess so Olivia deal."

"Just give me a minute go handle your business."

As I head to the bathroom I looked back and I could see that I now had him shook up not that that was my intentions but hey he asked for the truth right? By the time I came back to sit down.

"Ok lay it on me fuck it I need to know Olivia I came this far what's up? What's going on?"

"Ok well here goes. So one day, it was like any other regular day I came home from class Craig was at practice and I had made some popcorn and had a glass of lemonade then put on a movie in the living room. Anyways, I started to get real sleepy really fast out of nowhere next minute I know I wake up in the dark its pitch black I can't see a thing. My hands are tied to a chair that I'm sitting in and so are my feet so I begin to panic I scream, yell, cry, everything yelling for help I have no idea how long I was out for but it felt as if I were yelling and crying for hours yelling help, help, but nobody ever came to help me. But then out of nowhere I begin to hear footsteps coming closer in my direction so I begin yelling again "hey over here" help please god help me. As a light a very bright light flickers on and because I had been in the dark for so long and crying for so long I could barely see anything as the shadow approached me and got closer and closer I could finally make out who it was.

"Who was it?" Clarence asked.

"I couldn't believe it but it was Bernie the realtor and I was so happy that he found me. I said "oh my god Bernie thank god it's you" please help me, untie me please, where am I? Then he said laughing at me what do you mean where are you Olivia? You are home. I said what is so damn funny? Untie me what do you mean I'm home? To make a long story short after a while Clarence, I realized he was the one who put me there!"

"How do you know he was the one who put you there? And where were you at?"

"Because after a while he admitted to me that he wasn't there to help me he was there to torture and kill me." I continued,

"He said that he drugged me with lemonade he use to bring over which I also found in your house."

"So you are the one who broke into my house? I knew that was you Olivia, yeah he use to bring us that lemonade all the time I told the police that I wasn't staying there anymore but I came back the day after I guess you broke in to catch the suspect but they wouldn't let me stay there for real after that. So where did this sick fuck take you Olivia?"

"That's just the thing, I don't know but he kept saying that I was home which was weird though."

"Well how did you escape?"

"I didn't he let me go he said that I was his first."

"His first what? What does that mean?"

"His first victim I guess I'm not sure." I replied.

"Why would he let you go for Olivia? It doesn't make any sense?"

"Because he made me do some disgusting, degrading, and horrible things in order for me to live and leave. He threatened to kill my parents, friends, but most importantly Craig if I moved or told anyone about what took place that day and I kept that promise up until today so there you have it Clarence."

"Holy shit, Olivia I am so sorry but we have to go to the police let's talk to that Detective Ross guy he will believe us if you tell him what happened to you."

"Will he though?"

"Yes Olivia how could he not? This sick fuck has Maria and Angel we need to do something and put a stop to this maniac. Like what are we waiting for Olivia?"

"I know I tried to avoid this I don't want anyone to get hurt but you are right we have to put a stop to this guy so let's go talk to Detective Ross."

"Do you want to go see him now?"

"No, I will call him now and tell him that I need to speak to him that it's urgent."

"Ok cool, I will also call him so that he knows it's very urgent."

"Ok cool I will talk to you later be safe."

"Ok you too Olivia."

"Oh and by the way, I forgot to tell you that this guy took Craig out for beers the other night did you know anything about that?" I asked.

"Are you serious? No I don't go out with the guys not since Maria has been gone at least it just don't feel right you know?" Clarence replied.

"Yeah ok I understand, hey how is Anthony doing? He won't return a call or text of mine since the other day."

"He is doing ok I will talk to him for you ok?"

"That's ok, just tell him that I said hello and that I'm sorry."

"Ok Olivia, talk to you later."

And we went our separate ways. After that, I messaged Detective Ross but got no response. After twenty minutes or so, I decided to call him but still no answer. So I left a message on his voicemail. About a half hour later, he returned my call.

"Hey Miss. Mathis sorry it took me so long to get back to you what is the urgent news? Talk to me?" It sounded like he was in his car and extremely busy.

"Well, have you heard from Clarence yet?" I asked.

"Yes I just returned his phone call right before yours."

"Ok well what did he tell you?"

"He told me to call you that you have some information for me and that we all need to talk so here. I am speaking to you so now do you want to tell me what's going on please?" Detective Ross asked.

"When can we come to your office to speak to you in person Detective?"

"Well I am headed back to the office now so you can meet me now if you want to?" By this time it was already noon so I said,

"Sure thing I will see you in a few."

"So you are coming right?"

"Yes let me get a hold of Clarence and will be on our way."

"Great see you both soon."

After I hung up with the Detective, I called Clarence and he agreed to meet me at the police station to talk about what he and I discussed earlier in the day with Detective Ross. Once Clarence and I got to the station,

"Listen Olivia before we go in here and do this, are you sure you're ok with it?" Clarence asked.

"Yes I'm as good as I will ever be you know? I already told you plus he is around he found Craig at the grocery store. I mean enough is enough. I just hope they can find this guy and put him away so yes I am more than ready."

"Yeah me too Olivia me too. Do you think Maria and Angel are alive?"

"I hope so, I really hope so."

Once we got to Detective Ross office he looked exhausted like he hadn't slept in days. He told us both to have a seat like he usually did then asked us if we wanted a cup of coffee? We both declined the offer Clarence and I then Detective Ross sat down himself.

"Ok guys so what do you have for me?"

Clarence and I both looked at one another as he said,

"It's ok Olivia, take a deep breath and tell him it's ok."

"Ok well, I have a confession to make sir. I haven't been totally honest with you so here goes ok. You need to know something. I know who is responsible for all of this mess."

"You do? Ok well who is it Miss. Mathis?" Detective Ross asked. "It's the realtor."

"The realtor? You mean the realtor Burke Walters of that Master Realty Company? The guy you all bought homes from? That realtor?"

"Yes, him let me explain."

"Oh please do." Detective Ross said.

"Ok well one day after school, I went home like any other regular day I made myself some popcorn and sat in front of the television watching a movie drinking some lemonade. Anyways I began to get real hot and dizzy and sleepy and all of a sudden I wake up and I'm completely in the dark I have no idea what so ever where I am at but my hands are tied to the chair that I was placed in and so were my feet. So all I could do is yell and scream "help" "help" somebody please help me. I was terrified I had no idea what was going on it was pitch black I couldn't see anything so I just kept yelling then after a while I began to hear footsteps getting closer and closer so I began to yell louder and louder "in here" please god "I'm in here" help please the footsteps get closer and closer, louder and louder and then a door opens and these extremely bright lights come on as I'm saying to myself thank god someone found me. I could barely see because of the tears in my eyes and from being in the dark and asleep for so long that all I could see was a blurred image of what appeared to look like a man. As the person gets closer and closer I felt so relieved to see that it was the realtor Bernie but after a while I would realize that he wasn't there to help me but that he was the one who put me there."

"Put you where?" Detective Ross asked.

"That's the thing, I don't know where I was at but he kept telling me that I was home. I was in like a shed some kind of torture place I have no idea."

"How do you know he was the one who put you there?"

"What do you mean aside from the fact that he told me that he did by drugging me with the lemonade that I was drinking." I said.

"What lemonade?"

"He would drop off lemonade he made to people that he sold homes to something about his wife he would bring it to Maria as well right Clarence?" I asked Clarence.

"Yeah he was a weird guy. He would bring that shit to Maria all the time too." Clarence said.

"Ok so which one of you sent the glass and pitcher for prints?" Detective Ross asked.

"That was me sir, I also broke into Clarence place but that was only to get you the proof. Look this guy is sick he was going to kill me the only reason he didn't and let me go was because he tortured me and made me do sexual acts to him in order for me to leave." I said.

"How did you leave?"

"He drugged me again and when I woke back up, I was back on my couch as if it were all a bad dream. We need to catch this sick fuck!" as I began crying. Sobbing I continued,

"He said if I told anyone he would kill me and my boyfriend, you have to help us I know he has these girls somewhere please believe me."

"I do Miss. Mathis, look here is what we need to do. First, hey here is some tissue stop crying we will get this guy. Can you remember anything what so ever about where you were at? Anything helpful at all?" Detective Ross asked.

"Like I said, it was dark but once he turned on the lights it was a room, no windows, if so they were boarded up it looked like a shed of some sort. I remember the sound of water dripping it smelled musty like a work shed, there were all sorts of tools surgical scalpels it looked almost like a surgeon bought his tools to a shed to perform surgery. The room was white, only a chair in it with an old cloth on a table full of surgical equipment there were guns, knives, bats, scalpels, tools, it's like his torture place he must bring woman to."

"Ok tell me more about him telling you that you were home? What do you mean by that?"

"Well I kept yelling at him to untie me and to tell me where I was at and he kept laughing telling me that I was home that there was no need to worry and I would tell him no, I am not home where am I you sick fuck!?"

"And what else did he say?" As I see Detective Ross writing all this down on paper.

"Mostly he told me that I could yell and scream as loud as I wanted to that nobody could hear me that was about it."

"Well whoever this guy is, he is very smart a well-educated man he leaves no prints, the business cards are fake, the number is disconnected, and I'm willing to bet that his name is phony as well. So I could check on the number the last person to have it but I'm sure the name that came back would be fake." Detective Ross said.

"So what are we going to do?"

"Well I'm going to start with sending a team to all three of the homes. We will have to tear them apart from top to bottom looking for clues. In the meantime, you all may need to stay elsewhere if possible but if not, we still need to do a thorough search of all homes again. It is important that you all be very, very, careful because clearly we have a very sick man on our hands. Now, can you give me a very clear and detailed description of the Bernie guy please?"

"Sure, he is a tall middle aged white guy about 5'11 and weighs about 180 pounds black hair, no facial hair, no visible tattoos or piercing."

"Great what about eye color?" Detective Ross asked.

"Hazel, no wait, I think brown or black I don't know I think black."

"That was a lot of colors Miss. Mathis."

"I'm sorry, I'm pretty sure they are black, yes they are black."

"You are sure now?"

"Yes I am sure."

"Ok and lastly did he have a reason for why he kept bringing over this lemonade again?"

"Yes, he said that his wife who passed away loved to make lemonade so he does it in her honor or something like that."

"Ok got it all, I am on it, you both keep me informed about anything else you can remember or find out about this guy. In the meantime over the next few days me, and my team will be dropping by at each of your houses to see what we can find ok?"

"Ok." Clarence and I replied.

"Detective, I searched the entire house I found nothing." I said.

"Well sometimes, a fresh pair of eyes may help, now go on you both get to class and Olivia, thank you for telling me what you did I know that can't be easy to have to do but you have my word that we will find this guy ok?"

"You're welcome, ok Detective I sure hope so we need to find these woman."

As Clarence began to cry,

"I just want her back, please Detective she is my world. Please, I love her so much please just bring her back to me please god." Sobbing.

"I will son, I will do my best you have my word on that."

As Clarence and I sobbed, we stood up and hugged one another then shook Detective Ross hand as he escorted us out of his office. "I am so sorry for what you both have been through, but I can't stress it enough. This son of a bitch will make a mistake and when he does, I will be right there to put his sick ass away." Clarence and I replied,

"We hope so Detective." And left outside to the parking lot.

"Hey Olivia, I know it's really none of my business and all, but are you planning on telling Craig about any of this at all? Clarence asked.

"I don't know, I mean he told me that he would kill him if I did, but then again, he also said if I told anyone he would kill me and I've told you and the police already so I guess at this point I should tell him right?"

"It's just my opinion, but I think you should but that's just me."

"You're right, I think I will tell him tonight."

"Ok cool, well I have to get to class."

"Yeah me too." So we gave each other a hug and went our separate ways as we said to each other see you later be safe.

I finished up my school day like it was nothing. I was passing every test given to me despite getting barely any sleep because I was constantly pursing Bernie and these missing girls. Anyways, later on the night I called Craig to tell him that I was headed home but that I was going to make a quick stop at the grocery store to pick up dinner and wanted to know if he had any ideas.

"Umm it doesn't matter babe, whatever you want to make is fine by me. I'm starving can't wait to get home to eat. I'm sure whatever you make will be great but I have to go babe I love you." "Ok babe, I love you too talk to you later." And we hung up. There was a local grocery store around where we lived so I stopped there to pick up some steak and vegetables Craig loved steak and pork chops so I figured I'd surprise him and that's when the craziest thing happened to me.

As I was walking down an aisle I turned off of an aisle seven to go onto eight and the aisle was completely empty but it felt like as soon as I turned onto eight way down on the other end of aisle eight there stood Bernie. I was in total disbelief I was terrified I didn't know if I should run, yell, scream, it was like I was frozen stiff I couldn't move or anything as he just stood at the other end of the aisle starring down at me with a very dark and creepy stare almost as if he were possessed looking right through me as he stood there looking like he was blocking the aisle wearing a black suit standing with his hands in his pocket. What was even crazier is that he had no shopping cart what so ever, no basket, nothing as he continued to stand there just looking at me. I asked myself what should I do? I was so scared of this man. The only thing that I could think of was turning around and going to another aisle so that is what I did, but there he stood again this time only creepier because a man was in this aisle in the middle shopping as Bernie and I stood on both opposite ends of the aisle he continues to just stare at me like he was possessed. The man in the aisle shopped casually not noticing a thing, but being that he was there made me feel a bit relieved that

Bernie couldn't hurt me or anything like that. So I started to walk down the aisle and it was like Bernie was my shadow because as soon as I moved forward so did he. Now as we are both walking towards one another the random shopper begins to walk moving in the direction of Bernie as was I myself. Then I stop and act as if I am looking at something on a shelf Bernie continues past the gentleman and walks right up to me as my heart begins to race, I grab my cell phone as Bernie said,

"Do you really want to do that Olivia?"

"I will scream, don't touch me you sick fuck!" I repled quietly.

"No you won't and I'll tell you why, you're not going to do shit you fucking whore because then both of those little bitches will die, you remember your whore friends don't you?"

"They are still alive?"

"Well yes, for now they are, but you just killed one Olivia because I made the rules so simple how much clearer could I have made myself? I told you to keep your beautiful dick sucking mouth shut but no you had to be a dumb bitch and get innocent people killed didn't you?"

"I didn't tell anyone Bernie, I swear please don't kill anybody please."

"No you didn't tell anybody except for Clarence and Detective Ross of the mother fucking Los Angeles Police department you fucking bitch? Oh and my personal favorite the care package you sent the Detective. What is the problem with you whores huh? I tell you to do something and you do the opposite so now you forced my hand bitch. So who's it going to be huh? Angel? Maria? Craig? Detective Ross? Who is going to be first?"

As I try to keep my composure and not begin to cry, I plead with him as I'm still speaking quietly.

"Please don't do this Bernie, what do you want from me?"

"What makes you think that I want anything from you? This is about choices and bitch you made the wrong one."

"Please don't hurt them leave Craig alone."

"Oh yeah your faggot boyfriend precious fuck boy Craig you know I kind of like him we hung out but just because I like you better I will save him for last." As a tear began to fall down my face,

"You better wipe that shit now don't draw attention or make a sense." He said.

I wiped my face hoping the gentleman would notice but he walked right past us and minded his business. Bernie even went as far as to say hello to him as he past us in the aisle.

"Well it was nice seeing you again Olivia, you are beautiful as always," as he passes the back side of his hand across my cheek.

"I will be in touch, but like I said you didn't keep your end of the deal so now I have to keep my promise. I wish you would have just listened to me sweetheart."

"You are sick Bernie, you need help please tell me where they are?"

"They are home where they belong. Bye now what happens next Olivia is on your hands. Besides, I'm getting tired of this city I'm going back home soon."

"Where is home?" I asked him and he laughed.

"See you soon Olivia," as he walks away.

Bernie walks to his car gets in and begins to beat on the steering wheel hard as hell repeatedly screaming at himself,

"You are so fucking stupid, why did you do that?" As he continued to beat and hit on the steering wheel looking at himself in the rearview mirror saying you stupid fucking idiot now you know what you have to do. He said to himself in the third person. He yelled "fuck" then starts up the car and drives to the college after getting out his car. He looks around then ends up in a dark hallway. He hits a switch and a line of Christmas lights turn on as he walks down this hallway and opens a door screaming out loud

"Help please, help!" as a young girl continues to cry for help. Bernie yells back,

"Shut the fuck up you dumb bitch, nobody can hear you nobody knows where you are. You whore but guess what today is your lucky day."

The young lady still in a dark area unrevealed at this point crying asked,

"Why is that?"

Bernie replied,

"Because today is the day that I set you free," as he hits on another switch. We see now that it is Maria Cooper.

"Seriously? Are you for real?" She replied sobbing.

"Yes for real, I'm not happy about it. You can thank that bitch Olivia for telling your boyfriend, a detective, and god only knows who else, just so you know, I didn't want to do this."

Maria sobbing replied,

"Thank god, thank you so much Bernie for doing the right thing."

"Well you can say goodbye. Here is a phone, I want you to call your boyfriend Clarence and tell him goodbye."

"What for? You said you were letting me go?" She asked.

"Yes letting you go out of your misery," as he began to laugh, he said,

"Wait oh you thought I would let you go literally?" As he continued to laugh.

"What are you nuts or something? The only way you leave here now is dead, you can thank Olivia now for that."

As Maria begins to ball out crying, "Please Bernie don't do this please don't."

"Call Clarence say goodbye I'm giving you that much now don't piss me off Maria. Let's go, I have shit to do you know."

Maria begins to yell, "Help, help!" as Bernie walks over to her and smacks her in the face so hard.

"Look I am running out of patience, make the damn call it's now or never," as he handed her the phone. Maria grabs the phone sobbing hysterically and begins to dial Clarence's number as Bernie said, "Get a hold of yourself girl."

Dial tones goes off about six times before Clarence finally answered and heard a woman crying on the other end of the phone. "Oh my god, Maria baby is this you?" Clarence asked.

"Yes baby, I just wanted to tell you that I love you so much I don't know if I ever truly told you that enough." Clarence begins to cry and said,

"Yes baby you did, all the time. Come home please, I need you god I miss you so much." Clarence replied. Maria sobbed and responded,

"I wish I could, this is my goodbye to you, babe I want you to know how proud I am of you the time I spent with you was the best times of my life. You truly are and always will be the love of my life I'm so sorry."

Clarence cried and replied,

"Baby, don't be. Just come home I don't care why you left I love you, I just want you home back in my arms where you belong."

"I wish baby, I really wish I could." as Clarence interrupts and said,

"You were supposed to be my wife baby, kids and all, we were so close what happened?"

"I will always be with you babe, I'm your wife in spirit you go on and be that great football player that you were destined to be babe." Maria replied.

"No, not without you. Where are you babe? I'm coming to get you does that piece of shit realtor Bernie have you?"

"Hey Bernie if you can hear me, you sick fuck! The police are on to you so let my girlfriend go now please."

"I love you babe," as Bernie in the background said,

"That's enough! Your time is up. You two make me sick!"

Clarence yelled into the phone,

"Let her go bro take me instead man." Clarence begun yelling so loud that his teammates on the field could hear him yelling.

"Take me instead, please!" as Bernie walks up behind Maria as she is holding the phone.

"No Clarence, I'll take her instead" and shot Maria in the back of her head.

"No!!!!" Clarence yelled and then heard a dial tone as Maria dropped the phone. Clarence dropped to his knees as he balls out crying and yelling "no" please god help her. His teammates including Craig go over to Clarence to find out what was going on as he tells them,

"He killed her, he killed her! My Maria is gone he killed her!"

Bernie then begins to yell at Maria's dead body. See what Olivia made me do bitch? I didn't want to kill you not like this and look what she made me do? Now I must set a real example this is nuts. Bernie says as he continues to speak to Maria's dead body, now I have to get rid of your body I can't leave you here this is nuts.

Meanwhile when I got home, I was so nervous thinking that Bernie might have followed me home from the grocery store so I locked all my doors and waited on Craig to get home from football practice. I wanted to talk to him about what Bernie had did to me it was time to tell him I was such a nervous wreck that I couldn't even cook so I called him a few times but got no answer. When Craig finally got home that night he looked like he had seen a ghost and had a very long day as usual. I tried to not look stressed out so that he would be able to tell me about his day because if I ever looked stressed he wouldn't talk about his day he would just want to hear about mine. So when he walked in,

"Hey babe how was your day? hey listen we really need to talk it's very important."

"Ok but listen, today at the practice, Clarence got a phone call from the person who has his girlfriend Maria."

"Oh my god, are you serious? How do you know?"

"Because he got a call on his phone then just began screaming "no" "no" please god help her so we all rushed over to him and kept asking him what was going on? He just fell to his knees saying she is dead he killed her."

After Craig told me that, I fell to my own knees and began crying saying,

"Oh my god, this is all my fault." Craig ran over to catch me.

"No babe this has nothing to do with you, how could this possibly be your fault babe?" as he held me up and said,

"Don't cry, they will get whoever is responsible for this babe they will."

"Babe there is something that I need to tell you."

"What's up babe talk to me?"

"I know who is doing this, you have to trust me on this."

"Ok who is it babe?"

"It is our realtor, Bernie. Babe, he is a sick psychopath."

"Baby, what makes you think that he is responsible for all this? He seems like a decent guy to me?"

"Because it happened to me once before."

"What happened once before Olivia?"

"Listen babe, one day when you were at practice awhile back I was here at the house watching a movie like any other day. Well you know that lemonade that Bernie would always bring over for us?"

"Yeah what about it?"

"Well, I was drinking it while I sat on the couch and watched a movie and all of a sudden I begin to get hot and dizzy, very sleepy and I guess I passed out. Anyways I wake up in this pitch black room and I'm tied to a chair by my feet and wrist but to make a long story short I yell for help for god knows how long and when someone finally comes to my rescue its Bernie only he's not there to help me I later would find out that he is the one who put me there."

"Put you where?"

I get frustrated and said, "God damn that is what everyone keeps asking me, but I don't know, I have no idea where I was at."

"How do you know Bernie put you there?"

"Because he told me he did he also told me that he drugged me with the lemonade."

"What? Wait a second who all knows about this? And why does anyone know before me Olivia?"

"Detective Ross and Clarence know that's it."

"Babe I couldn't tell you because Bernie said if I told anyone especially you that he would kill me and you both."

"When did this happen?"

"Months ago, I wanted to tell you babe for so long I wanted to tell someone, anyone, I was so scared."

"How did you escape though?"

"He let me go…" as I began to cry even harder.

"He made me do things babe, sick things in order for my life and freedom." Craig was irate and began throwing objects as he said,

"Where can I find this piece of shit at?"

"Everything we know about him is fake, this is why nobody has been arrested yet."

"Babe, I fucking just hung out with this fucking guy are you kidding me? I wish you would have told me this a long time ago." Sobbing I said, "Babe, I couldn't I was protecting you I was protecting us."

"How did this prick get in here? Does he have a key or something?"

"I don't know babe, we all have been trying to figure this all out."

Craig is now pacing back and forth pissed scratching his head.

"Tomorrow we change all these fucking locks and why did you say him killing Maria was your fault?" Craig asked.

"Because I ran into Bernie tonight at the grocery store, I was so scared he has been following me and apparently you too. He said that he knew that I told Detective Ross and Clarence and that I didn't follow the rules so now he has to kill someone so I guess he killed poor Maria," as I began to ball out crying in tears.

"This guy is insane Craig, I'm so fucking scared." I said.

"Don't worry baby this sick fuck won't ever touch you again you got my word on that. Tomorrow we all need to go see this Detective Ross guy and find out what he is doing to find this guy ok."

"Ok babe I need to call Clarence."

"Ok I'm going to change, I need to take my shower are you ok?"

"Ok babe." As he came up to me and said,

"Listen Olivia, I would burn in hell to make sure you are safe don't worry now that I know this cocksucker wont fuck with us anymore trust me." Then he gave me a big hug and a kiss on the forehead.

"Don't worry, I love you."

"I love you too Craig, I'm so sorry for not telling you sooner."

"Don't apologize babe, you did the right thing. Then went to go take his shower.

I stayed in the kitchen and called Clarence but got no answer. I even tried to text him but no answer back so I left a voicemail and just waited. After showering and a long night of talking, Craig and I just called it a night and went to bed. That next morning Clarence had messaged me back saying that he didn't want to talk last night when I had been calling and messaging but that he would speak to me at school. He had also asked if I had spoken to Craig yet? I told him that I did and that we should all sit down and talk and that we all needed to speak to Detective Ross as well and he agreed so that morning I remember I called Detective Ross but he didn't answer so as I usually did I left a message. Craig left for school before me at 9:00 am I left for class around 10:00 am and saw that Craig had been calling me like crazy but my cell phone had been on vibrate so I didn't hear the call. But when I pulled up on campus there were cops everywhere, news camera crews, you name it, I had no idea what was going on I figured it was about what had happened to Maria. When I got out of my car, I immediately called Craig he picked up fast,

"Babe, I've been blowing you up did you hear yet what happened?"

"Yeah I know, I'm sorry babe I didn't hear it. I left it on vibrate what's going on? I see police everywhere?"

"Where are you Olivia?"

"In the parking lot why?"

"Listen, I guess this morning that theater teacher Professor Lucas found Maria's dead body hanging from the ceiling."

"Oh my god, are you serious?"

"Yeah I'm serious, this sick fuck how is he doing this?"

"I don't know, oh my god does Clarence know yet? Has he seen it?"

"I don't know yet, have you spoke to him yet?"

"Yeah but only through message, he said we would talk today." "Ok well, go straight to class if your even able to. I think school might be out today or I'm guessing just that class either way go to class or go home Olivia."

"I need to find Clarence this is so fucking bad, did you see her hanging?"

"No, but the Professor did, I think he and the police that's it."

"Why would Bernie put her in there, for it makes no sense though?"

"Because he is a sick psycho fuck there is no reason other than he is sick, babe what do you expect?"

"I guess you are right, but this guy is not stupid he is very smart, very calculated, so this is very weird even for him."

"No, he is just sick babe trust me."

As I began to walk to class through all the squad cars and camera crews in the parking lot, I saw a crowd of students talking about how they still don't know why Maria's body was placed there? And that her body still was hanging there in the class room. I was curious to know how all of these people knew what was going on in the classroom so I decided to walk over to the theater where Professor Lucas classroom was at. It was taped off by caution tape though and you couldn't see much of anything other than a crowd of people and cops everywhere. Clarence had called me and I picked up the phone so fast,

"Clarence I am so sorry about Maria what happened? Listen he has been stalking me I ran into him at the grocery store."

"He called me and had her tell me goodbye right before he killed her." Sobbing he continued,

"She was my everything Olivia she was all that I had left."

"I am so sorry Clarence where are you? Listen fuck school today, let's just meet at my place and talk what do you say?"

"God bless your heart Olivia, but I already saw it on the news. I'm headed there now to say goodbye to my lady."

"I don't think that is such a good idea, please don't."

"See you in a few," and hung up on me.

As I sat outside as a spectator like the rest of us in total disbelief, I saw Detective Ross and begun to yell,

"Hey Detective Ross!" as I rush up to the caution tape as officers rush to me and said,

"Ma'am, back up there is nobody allowed to pass this line, back up now please."

"Look my name is Olivia Mathis, Detective Ross is expecting me please," as one officer said,

"Ok wait here let me check."

He goes over towards Detective Ross as I then see them speaking for a minute then Detective Ross looks in my direction and waves for me to come over. Another officer closer to me lifts the caution tape and lets me through as I walk over to Detective Ross.

"What do you have for me Miss. Mathis, make it quick as you can see I'm very busy here?" He said.

"Ok I will, so listen. Clarence got a call from him yesterday night at practice telling Maria to say bye to Clarence then shot her he said."

"That would explain the bullet hole in the back of her head then."

"Listen, he also showed up at the grocery store and spoke to me yesterday night about an hour or two before he killed Maria."

"An hour or so you said?"

"Yes." I replied.

"He is local hints, they are home hmm."

"What are you talking about?"

"I need to speak to Clarence where is he?"

"He is on his way here sir."

"No he can't be here, tell him to meet at my office. I need to know what this guy spoke to you and him both about."

As I heard yelling in the background and Detective Ross yelled, "Stop him!" It was Clarence charging through the yellow caution tape as he yelled,

"Maria!" he rushes towards the room door where his girlfriend's body hung from the theater ceiling. Officers try to tackle him down to stop him from witnessing Maria's body but his massive build and football experience broke through and Clarence whipped open the door to the theater as you then see Maria's body still hanging from the ceiling. She looked like she had lost so much weight and was wearing the same clothes that she had been wearing from the last time anyone had seen her. Clarence yelled,

"Cut her down you fucking assholes, cut her the fuck down!" as Detective Ross tries to calm Clarence down Detective Ross yelled,

"Close that damn door now."

Officers close the door as Clarence falls to the ground yelling, "Maria, oh god!"

I go over and hug him as we both are in tears saying to him,

"Maria is in a better place now Clarence nobody can hurt her now she is in peace."

As we are both sitting on the ground, Clarence said to me'

"He made me listen to him shoot her."

"What?"

"He made me listen to him shoot her!"

"We are going to catch him Clarence. Listen to me, let's get up and go to Detective Ross office and tell him about your phone call and I will tell him about my conversation with Bernie in the grocery store ok? Craig even wants to talk to him about his experience with this scumbag. We all need to help these police find this guy he still has Angel and god only knows who else."

Clarence trying to get a hold of himself said,

"You are right Olivia, let's do that because I've had enough. I don't know how much more of this that I can take."

I helped Clarence get up and told him,

"It should all be over really soon."

Detective Ross came from back out of the theater and said,

"You all can leave your vehicles here and come with me now." So we all jumped into Detective Ross's vehicle and he drove us off campus back to the police station when we got there I called Craig to tell him to come over as well. We sat down in his office but I remember the walk from the vehicle to the building how many people were outside the station news crews trying to snap photos of Clarence and what not it was just crazy and unreal to me. Once in Detective Ross's office we sat there and he said,

"Damn, I am so sorry Clarence no words can describe how sorry I am but I'm going to need you to tell me about that phone call so we can catch this prick you understand me?"

"Yeah I do." Clarence replied.

"Ok good. Before we start, can I get you all anything to eat or drink?"

"No thank you sir," We both replied.

"Ok so what happened at practice that night Clarence?"

"Nothing, we were in the middle of drills and my cell goes off. I could hear it on the bench so I ran up to it thinking that any day it could be my baby Maria." As Clarence fights back tears he continued to say,

"So I look at it and it says "unknown caller" so I answer it and to my surprise, I hear another voice on the other end of the phone a woman crying and I knew it was Maria. So I said Maria baby is that you? She said yes and goes on to tell me how much she loves me and it was like her telling me goodbye or something. Then Bernie took the phone and said that is enough we make him sick then I heard a gunshot and a dial tone that's it."

"And you know for sure it was this Bernie guy?"

"Look, I know dude's voice. It was 100% percent him."

"This guy is good, blocking the number but we will try to trace where the call was made from anyway, but it will be difficult though. Any background noise?"

"No, just an echo that's about it."

"Ok Miss. Mathis, it's your turn. What do you have for me?"

"It's all my fault that Maria is dead that's what Bernie told me."

"What do you mean by that?" as now I am also fighting back tears,

"He has been following me this entire time, he was in the grocery store following me. He came up to me and said that I broke the rules by telling you and Clarence about what happened to me so he said now he has to keep his promise and kill someone I plead with him not to. He said you Detective or Clarence or one of the two girls now have to die that's when I knew that they were still alive but then he left I guess shortly after he killed Maria. Clarence I am so sorry I really am."

"Why didn't you call the cops Olivia?"

"He would have been gone before they showed up plus I was terrified, I'm so sorry Clarence and I told you if I spoke what he would do to us."

"Ok we will get surveillance from the grocery store inside and the parking lot let's hope he drove. What is the name of the grocery store that you were in when this took place and what time was it around?"

"It was at Ralph's and it was around 5:30 pm maybe 6:00 pm or so."

"Ok good, were getting somewhere." Then Detective Ross's door opened and Craig and Anthony walked in.

"Hello Anthony and you must be Craig I take it?" Asked Detective Ros.

"Hello Detective, hey Clarence man I'm so sorry bro," as he hugs Clarence. Craig said,

"Yes sir that's right." And also gives his condolences to Clarence as well.

"Ok now that we are all here together, what else do you all have for me?" The detective asked.

"Well a few days ago after practice, I stopped at a grocery store and ran into this Bernie guy he says hello how have you been and what not? Craig said and continued,

"Then he offered to buy me and the guy's beer. He sais that he hasn't been out in a while so it's cool. So we let him and he seemed like a pretty cool dude granted I didn't know he was a sick maniac at this point that's about it."

"Ok what grocery store was it, what was the name of the bar you went to?"

"Ralph's that was the grocery store and Rocco's Tavern was the name of the bar we were at." Craig said.

"Ok and times please?"

Craig said grocery store was at maybe 6:00 pm and the bar was till about 6:30 or 7:00 pm.

"I will follow all there leads, and see what comes up that's all we can do for now guys we are doing all we can but first I need to find out why he put her body in Professor Lucas classroom?"

"Ask him and his helper Dennis."

"I will do that Miss. Mathis, thank you. Ok so anything else anyone? Detective Ross replied.

"Yeah please find Angel." Anthony said.

"We are doing all we can son. Ok so if nothing else let me get on this I have a lot of work to do. Thank you all for coming in now let me do what I do best and catch this prick."

As we all cleared out of the Detectives office and went our separate ways, Detective Ross went to go question Professor Lucas about what he saw that morning. Detective Ross goes back into the classroom.

"Hi Professor Lucas is it?"

"Yes can I help you?" Professor Lucas replied.

Detective Ross then flashes his badge and said,

"Yes I hope. So my name is Detective Eric Ross, I am a homicide Detective for the Los Angeles Police Department amongst other things. This is your classroom right?"

"Yes it is."

Detective Ross continued to say,

"You are the only teacher that teaches in this classroom correct?, Nobody else?"

"Yes, that is correct."

"Ok can you tell me about what happened this morning?"

"Nothing, I opened up my door and there she was, I jumped and called 911."

"Does anyone other than yourself have access to this room?"

"Nobody but the janitor that I know of."

"Ok. Hmm you know what I find very strange about this Professor Lucas?"

"No what is that Detective?"

"It's the fact that there are hundreds of classrooms on this campus why pick yours to leave her body at? Don't you find that to be strange Professor? Professor Lucas replied yes

"Yes I do, in fact it's very strange I thought that myself as well." "And what did you come up with?"

"Excuse me?"

"Well why do you think her body was placed here? Out of everywhere else on earth, the killer could have placed her body why here?"

"I have no idea Detective, I thought that was your job to determine?" Professor Lucas replied.

"Yeah I guess so Professor. Nevertheless, here is my card if you hear anything or think of anything you give me a jingle ok?"

"I sure will Detective, oh and hey by the way, do you all have any suspects or leads on anything?"

"Well, I certainly couldn't give that information to you professor. You're just going to have to watch the news like everyone else, but thank you for your time. I will be in touch Professor."

"You are welcome Detective, sorry I couldn't be more of assistance to you."

"That is ok. Oh by the way Professor, your classroom is now a crime scene so class is out."

Then Professor Lucas temperament changed from nice guy to pissed off as he yelled,

"Oh great, that's just great, someone puts a corpse in my classroom and now I'm out of work? Thank you so much for your help Detective."

"That will be enough Professor," as a young man came over to the Professor with a glass of water and a prescription bottle of pills. "Calm down Professor, here are your pills. Here take it and calm yourself down. The Detective is just doing his job. Sorry sir he gets like this when he gets upset."

"Who are you?" The young man reached to shake my hand,

"Oh I'm sorry how rude of me, my name is Dennis, Dennis Hathaway, I am the Professors assistant."

"Oh yes, ok Dennis just the man I wanted to speak to, do you have a moment?"

"Sure, how can I help you Detective?"

"Tell me a little bit about your relationship with the Professor as he remembered Miss. Mathis told me to speak with Dennis and I also could admit that the Professor's attitude and behavior rubbed me the wrong way as well."

"I am a film student, a student of acting, I help the Professor with the class when he is running late by instructing the other students on what to do and what not."

"Do you have keys to the classroom?"

"No I don't."

"Well, how do you let the students in the classroom when the Professor is running late then?"

"Umm Professor?" Dennis looks to the Professor.

"I'm asking you Dennis, not the Professor?"

"Tell him it's ok." Said the Professor.

"I call him if he is late, I go meet him to get the keys to open up the classroom."

"That sounds weird, is that even allowed?"

"Yes it is, are we done here Detective?"

"Yes one more thing though, what medication do you take Professor?"

"I take Klonopin for my anxiety, are we done now?"

"Yes for now, we will be in touch. Have a good one gentleman." Detective Ross then left the crime scene in the classroom and goes all the way to the football field to speak to the coach and a couple of the players on what they might of saw regarding Bernie. The Detective walks up to a man on the field.

"Hello Coach Davis is it?"

"Yes, how can I help you Detective? Coach Davis said.

"Well, I was wondering if you had seen a gentleman a few days ago walk onto this field and began speaking to one of your players at all?"

"In fact I did, a tall guy about 5'11 or so wearing a black suit walked up onto the field and started talking to Craig my quarterback. You might want to speak to him about it. I don't know what was said though. Why do you ask?"

"Well, because that man is a person of interest. That's all. How long did they speak for?"

"I'm not sure really." One of the players nearby walked up interrupted the conversation and said,

"He showed up at Ralph's too, Craig told me then he even showed up at Rocco's and bought all of us drinks."

"Ok so do you know how long they spoke for?"

"Yeah about five minutes or so I remember Craig asked him what he was doing here and the guy said he was looking to buy more property and came by to just say hello which Craig found to be pretty weird." The player said.

"Ok thank you for your time gentleman."

"You're welcome Detective." Both Coach Davis and the player said.

Now Detective Ross was headed to the bar that the boys drank at that night. When the Detective got there, he spoke to a guy named Mark who was the manager of the bar. Detective Ross walks in sits at the bar casually and orders a coke and flashes his badge as he said, "After you get the coke, can you get the manager as well honey thanks?"

"Yeah sure." The bartender said.

Then about five minutes later, the manager comes out this tall muscular guy.

"Hi my name is Mark I am the manager here, how can I help you Detective?"

"Well I guess we are about to find out Mark," and continued.

"The UCLA football team comes here a lot after their practices?"

"Yeah they do."

"Ok so would you say that you know most of them by name? That all or most are familiar faces?"

"Yes I can, for the most part, yeah you could say that."

"Ok so you would recognize an unfamiliar face quick I assume right?"

"Sure would."

"A few nights ago, the team came in here and a gentleman wearing a black suit and tie came in with them and paid for their drinks, does this ring a bell at all Mark?"

"Hell yeah, I remember that guy what was his name again? Bernard or something like that?"

"Bernie?"

"Yeah Bernie, cool dude and a great tipper too."

"Yeah I bet, listen I'm going to need his bill, credit card information, all of that now please ok?"

"Oh no he didn't pay with a card, he paid the bill in cash which I found to be weird considering the bill was so high but hey money is money you know what I mean?"

"Fuck this prick is good," as he lights up a cigarette.

"Why, what did he do?"

"Mark do you have surveillance throughout your bar? Please tell me that you do?"

"Sure do sir."

"That's great news Mark, I'm going to need the tape from that night oh and his bill as well."

"Great coming right up sir give me a minute."

"Take your time man."

About five minutes later Mark came back with the tape and receipt. "Thank you very much Mark for your help and time here is my card. My name is Detective Eric Ross contact me if you think of any useful information regarding that night. And more importantly if you see Bernie again call me immediately ok?"

"Ok but are you going to tell me what he did? You think he kidnapped those women?"

"Mark at this point, he is just simply a person of interest that's all ok."

"Ok Detective."

"Ok again, thank you for your help and time have a nice day," as he put out his cigarette.

Then from there Detective Ross head to Ralph's the grocery store that Bernie confronted both myself and Craig at. When Detective Ross got there he went straight to the front desk and asked for the store manager. The young lady store clerk went to get her manager then came back out without the manager and asked, "Um he is busy, what is this regarding sir?"

Detective Ross flashes his badge and said this is what its regarding please tell him to make time. The store clerk runs back into the office and tells the manager,

"Sir sorry to bother you again, but the gentleman who asked for you out there is a cop. As the manager jumps up and says "Oh shit, ok tell him I will be right out. The store clerk goes back out the office,

"Ok officer my manager said that he will be right out, sorry about that."

"That's no problem dear not your fault, thank you."

"You're welcome." The store clerk said and left.

When the manager of Ralph's came out, he was extremely nervous as if the Detective was there for him or something and very scared. "Hi I am the manager, my name is David how can I help you officer?"

"How are you doing David? I need surveillance from within the store and out from about a week ago, last week that is."

"Ok, I can do that officer and what's this in regards to because I didn't report any incident?"

"I am just here simply following leads on an open case that's all." David looking relieved said, "Oh ok cool, I will get that for you, do you need it now?"

"Yes, now would be great sir."

"Ok just give me a minute and I will grab that for you let me just run into the office, In fact here just come with me."

As the Detective follows David into his office David,

"Go on and take a seat."

"No that is ok, I will stand thank you," as David then hands over the tape.

"Ok you're all set their officer. Can I be of any more help to you?" "Nope, that will be it David, thank you for your help I appreciate it."

"No problem sir anytime."

It was time for the Detective to head back to the office to review these tapes but before doing so he needed to call me about Craig. He dialed my number and I picked up right away.

"Tell me something good Detective?"

"Listen, does Craig have any reason to lie to you about the realtor Bernie?"

"No way, why do you ask that?"

"Well Coach Davis and another player says that they saw Craig talking to Bernie at practice at Ralph's and at

Rocco's. He never mentioned speaking to him at practice that's why. So talk that over with him and call me back soon as possible ok?"

"Ok detective I will."

Later on that night once Craig got home from practice. I asked him

"Hey babe, did you speak to Bernie at practice that day you ran into him at the grocery store at all?" I asked him.

"Yeah, I told you that babe."

"No you told me you ran into him at the store then he met with you all at the bar nothing about practice."

"Ok well my bad, it must have slipped my mind I'm sorry babe who told you anyways?"

"Detective Ross spoke to your coach now he is curious to know why you didn't tell him?"

"Oh well yeah he is weird he showed up there talking about how he was looking for new property and that he just stopped by to say hello but now I know he is a sick stalker."

"Ok because now I have to tell the Detective this babe ok?"

"That's fine babe, my fault I'm sorry."

"I said its ok babe, I trust you."

That next morning, I called Detective Ross and told him what Craig had said. He told me that everything was ok because what Craig told me collaborated with what the Coach and teammates had told him as well. Detective Ross also told me that things were heading in the right direction as far as the case is concerned and that he and the Los Angeles Police Department were going to make a major announcement regarding the case very soon. So throughout my day, I was just curious to know what they were going to say. I was hoping that they caught Bernie or found Angel and this would all be over. The Detective is now in his office and plays the surveillance tape from the bar Rocco's it shows the teammates walking in and sitting at the bar and now the Los Angeles Police Department finally has an image of Bernie so Detective Ross is running it through the database to see if his picture comes up. Then he looks over the surveillance of Ralph's grocery store while Bernie stalked me and Craig and even got video surveillance of the parking lot which will show the vehicle he was in if they got really lucky. I wonder what Detective Ross is about to announce? Later on that day everyone was watching the television weather it was on an actual television or on a cell phone it was like everyone was tuned into this major announcement do to air at 6:00 pm. I was at home watching the television and when it hit 6::00 pm their was a podium right outside of the police department with a lot of news reporters and microphones. Then out from the front door comes Detective Ross as he walks right up to the podium with confidence as cameras begin to flash,

"Good evening to the city of Los Angeles, my name is Detective Eric Ross of the Los Angeles Police Department crime division. In the murder and disappearance cases of Maria Cooper and Angel Clause we are pleased to announce that through investigative work we now have a prime suspect. Although he is still at large, we hope to have him real soon. This is a sketch of our guy he goes by Bernie or Burke Walters. He poses as a realtor here in the Los Angeles area so please be advised that this man is armed and extremely dangerous. Now, I will take a couple of questions before I go. As pandemonium breaks out and cameras begin to flash "Detective Ross"

"Detective Ross," the other woman Angel Clause, is she still alive? "I couldn't say at this point." Detective Ross replied.

"How is he getting these woman?" Another reporter asked.

"Well my investigation leads me to believe that he is drugging these woman with Lemonade, he brings new home owners that buy from him Lemonade that he drugs." Another reporter asks,

"Hi Detective Ross, my name is James Rent from the Los Angeles Post, lemonade you say? That seems very crazy how does he get in these homes sir? Does he have a key?"

"We are still in the middle of the investigation that's all folks, I have to go. Thank you all for your time."

"Wait Detective Ross, one more question please."

"No, that's all for now folks," and turned around and walked back into the building.

"Great that's just fucking great you see that bitch? Bernie yelled at Angel as she sits tied to a chair by her hands and feet.

"What do you want from me?" as she is crying hysterically.

"Please leave me alone and let me go please she said."

"You can thank that whore Olivia it's because of her, now that I have to hurt you."

As Angel begins to cry even harder and yelled,

"Why, who the fuck is Olivia?" Bernie replied by grabbing Angel by her face extremely hard and said,

"Look bitch!" as he shows her his cell phone with a live feed showing the news.

"I'm all over the fucking six o clock news when all she had to do was mind her fucking business that fucking bitch. Well Angel here is the deal, you and I are going to play a little game and the game is called "some dumb bitch has to die" and I'm going to allow you to choose who that is ok. The rules are very simple if you want to leave here ok sweetie?"

Angel continued to cry and said,

"Listen Bernie, if you let me go I won't tell them that you had me ok I promise."

"Oh no, you won't huh?" Bernie said and continued,

"Well what would you say considering I'm the prime suspect?

"No, I will tell them that I ran away that I didn't want to be with Anthony anymore."

"Huh and you would do all that for little old me? Just for me to let you go? Bernie asked.

"Yes, I will. I know you didn't want to do this like you said, it's all Olivia's fault anyways right?"

"Huh you make a strong point, let me think about it some."

Bernie walks over to table with weapons and objects on it and grabs a tiny surgical knife then walks back over to Angel as Angel begins to yell Bernie.

"What are you doing? Oh my god," as Bernie puts his left finger over his lips.

"Shhhhhhh." Bernie then takes his right hand holding the knife grabs Angel by her face again and begins to cut off her left ear as she is screaming in agony and blood begins to flow everywhere. "Oh my god, Bernie please stop !!!! You are hurting me please stop !!!!"

Bernie holding Angels left ear all bloody in his right hand.

"I cut your ear off bitch because you don't listen so I assumed you wouldn't miss it," as he begins to laugh with a very creepy and sadistic laugh. Then smiling as he begins to suck on the bloody ear.

"Wow, I love the taste of fresh blood, how about you Olivia?" Angel screamed in agony.

"My name is Angel! You sick fuck, I'm not Olivia please stop !!!! Please."

"You see, I don't get you dumb college whores. You all are supposed to be smart? You see all you have to do is listen so now for your offer my answer is a big "No." In fact, fuck no so now back to the game bitch."

As angel is bleeding pretty bad and getting very dizzy,

"You better not die on me bitch, you die when I tell you that its ok to die."

"Fuck you! No, I'm sorry I didn't mean that."

"Ok so here are the rules. You are going to pick one person to take your spot in that chair and here are the contestants. Number one is your bitch boyfriend Anthony? Or number two that cocksucker Detective Ross? Number three Clarence? Or number four Craig?, You decide who goes. It's simple. You pick one name, I go get them and then you my dear are free to go but time is ticking you must pick fast."

"You are sick Bernie, you need help I can help you please let me help you?"

"Right now Angel, you need to be more concerned with helping yourself sweetheart not me. I am in total control.

"You are sick, where is your mother at?" Bernie in a rage turned around walked up to Angel very fast as she began to scream and grabbed her hand and ripped her finger back so fast breaking it as Angel screams so loud.

"Don't you ever mention my mother again you fuck whore, have I made myself clear?"

Angel cried hysterically.

"Yes I am so sorry Bernie."

Bernie then comes right out of his rage as if none of that just had happened.

"Ok are you ready to pick a name now very calmly?"

"Yes I am."

"Great!"

I remember just watching that television in awe. A part of me was relieved then the other half of me was like "Wow" he is going to come after me and Craig now what have I done? Then I began to get these strange messages from Clarence saying that he quit the team today. I said Clarence don't quit just take time off to heal I know that there is nothing that I can say to make any of this better but they are on to him now they will catch him. Clarence replied by saying catching him won't bring back Maria I got this house for us not for me to sit in it alone. I replied I understand Clarence but time heals all wounds. Clarence replied hey thanks for being a good friend Olivia you and Craig. All I have left is Maria's dog bones can you and Craig keep him for me please? I won't need him anymore not where I'm going. I replied where are you going Clarence? You are beginning to scare me now? I continued to say you keep your dog and raise it until you're an old man it will be a reminder of Maria for you. Then I decided to call him because his messages were scaring me.

"Are you ok Clarence? Do you need me to stop by? We can talk?" "No that's ok Olivia take care hon. No wait!!!!! Hey, I'm coming over ok?" Clarence hung up the phone.

I said to myself shit!!! And I tried calling him back but he wouldn't pick up the phone.

"Oh my god, what should I do I said to myself?"

As Clarence sits in his living room chair, holding a picture of himself and Maria both, he places it on the coffee table in front of him as he kisses it.

"I miss you so much babe, I'm coming to be with you sweetie," as banging comes from the front door.

"It's Olivia, Clarence open up please!!!!!!!! It's me Olivia!!!! Let's talk ?????"

Clarence ignored her and picked up a knife as he begun to cry.

"Oh god." A noise comes from behind him as Clarence says out loud,

"I knew you would come for me," and a gun cocks,

"It's Bernie."

"You did, did you?" Bernie said.

"Well she picked you," with a sinister smile on his face repeats,

"She picked you son."

"I have no idea what you are talking about, but you are too late."

"Yeah why is that?" Bernie asked.

"Because of this," as he reveals to Bernie the knife that he is holding to his wrist.

"It's never too late son," as he pulls out a gun to shoot Clarence but before he could pop off a shot, Clarence slit his own wrist as blood began to flow all over the living room carpet from his wrist.

"No!!!!!!!!! Fuck you!!!!!!!" and still shot Clarence in the back of his head anyways just for good measure.

Meanwhile on the outside of the house, I heard a gunshot go off. "Clarence no!!!!!!!!!" I yelled as I looked for an object to bust out a window with. Once I finally found a big rock, I threw it through the glass front window then climbed in the house to find Clarence laying in the chair with blood still running down his wrist. I fell to the ground and just began to cry yelling at him Clarence why did you do that?????? Why????? I then called Detective Ross to tell him what had happened. When the cops finally arrived o felt like I had been questioned fifty times or more about what had happened. Craig showed up immediately once I called him and told him about what took place. It became another mob sense outside only this time I was in the middle of it but I didn't want to be on the news or television for fear of my life. Detective Ross got there and said to me ok Olivia I'm sure you have had to tell this story a million and one times now but I assure you that this will be your last time doing so but can you please tell me what happened? I said as I balled out in tears I was at home watching the news when I began getting weird messages from Clarence they were like goodbye messages they were strange. So I tried calling him but he wouldn't answer me again so I messaged him "does he want me to come over to talk" he messages me back saying goodbye Olivia take care. So I rushed over to his place to talk to him but he wouldn't open then all of a sudden I heard a gun shot go off so I broke his window and found him like that. Detective Ross replied ok let me get in here and see what's going on I'm going to need you both to hang tight as Craig consoles Olivia. Detective Ross walks into the house and seeing other Los Angeles Police Department officers and Emergency medical technicians around the body as he says to them ok gentleman what do you have for me? An officer replied we have a 25 year old male with laceration to the wrist and a gun shot wound to the back of the head. Detective Ross replied laceration to the wrist did you just say? The officer replied yes sir right here check it out for yourself. The Detective takes a look and says I was told he had shot himself? The officer replied no sir he didn't shoot himself he cut his wrist. The Detective said ok well who the fuck shot him then? The officer says I have no idea Detective because there is no signs of a break in and the victim was shot in the back of the head. Detective Ross replied by saying search this entire house and area someone else was in this house because he certainly didn't shoot himself in the back of his fucking head fuck man!!!! As he kicks over a chair next to him. Detective Ross walks back outside again to speak to Olivia and Craig and says listen you both shouldn't stay at home I think this guy has a key or some kind of access to your house. He continues to say Clarence was shot in the back of his head and his wrist was slit someone else was in that house Olivia did you see anyone at all? I said no sir nobody at all. I was looking through the front door and the front window but couldn't see anything really at all. Detective Ross replied ok I want you both to leave but I suggest that you all don't stay home this guy was in Clarence house today because the gun shot wound is from the back of his head. Detective Ross walks back into the house and says get a blood examiner over here to the officers now. He continues we have a long night ahead of us oh and you go get me a cup of coffee black no sugar as he tells a local officer to go do. Craig and I left back home and once we got there Craig said to me I'm not leaving home Olivia we are fine I'm not scared of Bernie if he comes in here he should be scared of me do you understand? I said yes baby this is not a game though this is a very sick man here that we are dealing with do you understand? Craig replied I do and I don't think this is a game but you have to understand that he is a regular guy he bleeds like the both of us I will go buy a gun first thing tomorrow morning and keep it in the house and we already changed the locks we are ok Olivia. I replied ok Craig I guess you are right babe. Meanwhile elsewhere Bernie walks back into the room where he has Angel at and begins to yell out loud fuck!!!! Fuck!!! Fuck!!!! Stupid son of a bitch!!!!!! you fucked up. Angel replied by saying I did what you asked I'm free to go right? Those are the rules right? Bernie replied well yes and no and for that I am truly sorry. Angel says but wait you said if I picked someone you would let me go? As she begins to cry again she says you promised. Bernie says yes I know but you see their was a problem and unfortunately that's not good for you. Angel sobbing replied Bernie what does that mean? Bernie replied well I killed him but I didn't so that changes the rules of the game. He continues you see this weak little fucking pussy took his own life can you believe that? A damn football jock he took his own life. I mean what the fuck right? In frustration mocking Clarence Bernie begins to say "oh my Maria" I miss you so much, I'm coming to be with you, what a fucking pussy he slit his own wrist. Bernie laughing says I wish he would of called me I would of done it for him but you know I still had to get credit for some of it so I still shot the prick but needless to say I don't get credit for that which means neither do you Angel I'm sorry the game has to continue. As Angel continues to cry saying but you promised that wasn't my fault Bernie please let me go. Bernie says well hey we both got robbed on that one but I do have a surprise for you. Angel replied by saying I don't want a surprise I want to go home Bernie please? Bernie says I've told you over and over again that you are home don't piss me off Angel. Angel says no my real home. Bernie replied by saying you are at your real home now back to the game who will it be next? Anthony? Detective Ross? Craig? Who shall our lucky winner be? Sobbing Angel replied you are sick please stop please. Bernie replied by saying or would you rather have the surprise? Angel says if its not my freedom its not a surprise. Bernie replied well what about a cellmate? Angel replied what do you mean a cellmate? Bernie says well I know it has to be lonely in here by yourself so what if I gave you some company here? He continues that way you have someone to talk to and what not? Angel replied you know what Bernie go to hell, fuck you, do what you want to do your just going to kill me in the end anyways right? Bernie says yeah you need company I can tell you are very stressed out. As if he didn't hear anything that Angel had just said to him Bernie turns around and walks to the door and says I'll be back soon sit tight I'll have some food for you too see you later as he slammed the door shut. Meanwhile back at Clarence's place a blood splatter expert came by and determined that Clarence had cut his wrist first this was the cause of death and said that someone standing behind him shot him in the back of the head after he was already dead. Detective Ross says ok so their defiantly was someone else in here with him? Did you boys find anything out yet? An officer says no sir their are no signs of a break in or forced entry what so ever the shooter had to have some type of access to the house and let themselves in or the victim let the shooter in himself sir. The officer continues we did a sweep of the entire house and nothing has been disturbed other than the front window sir. Detective Ross replied ok fuck!!! Thank you your free to go I will take it from here. The officer replied ok boss man. I went back over to Clarence's house to ask the Detective about Clarence's dog bones, I knew he wanted me to have it and I wanted to respect his last wishes. When I got there Detective Ross looked so stressed he must of gave a thousand interviews to the press and they were shitting all over him because it had been weeks without any arrest whatsoever. I walked up and said Hi Detective sorry to bother you but I was wondering what you all are planning on doing with Clarence and Maria's dog bones? Detective Ross said what dog are you talking about Miss. Mathis? there is no dog in there not as far as I know of why do you ask though anyways? I said well I only ask because in his text messages to me he asked me to keep his dog for him and I want to honor those wishes he was my friend and I feel a bit responsible for his death as well. Detective Ross replied ok I will look in there for a dog but I don't think there is one in there though. He continues to say and by the way you are not responsible for Clarence death its that psycho Bernie who should be and I will catch him if it's the last thing that I do. Detective Ross than tells me to wait outside as he goes back into the house to look for Clarence dog. I see the coroner taking Clarence's body out of the house this was so surreal to me this was like something out of a movie I just couldn't believe that he was gone. Detective Ross looked all inside and around Clarence place but found no dog then asked me are you sure he had it here? I replied no I'm not sure but where else would it be? He said it was his and Maria's dog. Detective Ross replied ok well will keep an eye out but nope there was no dog in there Miss. Mathis. I said ok well how did Clarence die? Detective Ross replied Olivia you sure that you didn't see anybody else in or around this house? I said yes I am sure why? Detective Ross replied by saying because Clarence was shot like you said but he didn't shoot himself someone else did. I said what do you mean? Bernie right? Detective Ross said I'm sure of it Clarence cut his wrist to take his own life so that shot you heard came after he did that which tells us someone else was in that house Olivia. The cause of death will not be for sure until a few days but as of right now that's what its looking like so will see though he said. I replied it was Bernie I know it was him. Detective Ross said ok go home Miss. Mathis let me handle this ok? I said ok Detective you will let me know if you find out right? Detective Ross replied yes I will. Elsewhere Bernie opens back up the door to where he has Angel and says ok Angel are you ready for your surprise? Angel sobbing says please let me go Bernie please? I'll do anything you say please? Bernie replied by saying I have this gift for you do you want it or not? Angel pleading with Bernie said please Bernie let me go!!!!!! Please!!!!!. Bernie says you are really starting to piss me the fuck off as he begins to march over to Angel very fast with a bag in his hand. Angel yells no!!!!! please stop!!!!! Ill take the gift. Bernie stops and says ok then great here goes but first close your eyes. As angel continues to cry and says no why? Now Bernie very angry says now I'm going to have to punish you bitch that is very rude to not except a gift that someone is trying to give to you. Angel replied no wait please!!! I will take it I'm sorry what is it? Bernie continues to say ok Angel this is your last time now close your mother fucking eyes now!!!!! As he yells. As angel sobbing closes her eyes Bernie holding a dirty big brown bag opens it and pulls out a white puppy and says "surprise" you can open your eyes now. Angel opens her eyes and continues to cry. Bernie then says see now you are not alone I thought that you would be happy aren't you? Angel sobbing says Bernie I am happy thank you can I eat now please? Bernie replied oh yes I got some burgers as he unwraps one and feeds it to her as the puppy runs around the room. Angel asks Bernie where did you get this dog from? Bernie says why does it matter? Angel replied well I guess it doesn't thank you for the food and the dog but I think I'm ready to continue playing the game now. This excites Bernie as he replied with a huge smile on his face really? Angel replied yes really I even know who I want you to go after Bernie. Bernie says I'm so happy for you right now see you are learning the rules of the game and embracing them way to go Angel. He then says so who will it be? Angel replied well I think nobody innocent should die and their is one person who isn't innocent but I keep noticing that their name is never mentioned on your list why is that Bernie? Bernie says "oh yeah" and who might that be Angel? Angel replied well the person you say is responsible for all of this I want you to take out that girl Olivia. Bernie replied by saying oh no that is out of the question pick someone else. Angel replied why not her? Bernie very angry says look you little bitch I don't answer to you the answer is fuck no!!!!!! further more she is last if even at all. Angel replied but why? You bitch about her all the time if she is why I'm really here then I choose her to take my place in this chair that's my pick. Bernie says well the answer is "no" so lets move on, I think her boyfriend Craig should be next he is a bitch anyways he doesn't deserve her. Angel replied "oh so I see now" why you wont kill her, why you are always upset about her, your fucking obsessed with her aren't you? You sick twisted fuck. Bernie walks over real fast up to Angel as she yells help!!!!! And slaps the shit out of her and says maybe I say fuck it and kill you now how about that you ungrateful little cunt? Now shut the fuck up before you piss me off as he grabs another one of her fingers and Angel yells no wait please!!!!! Bernie ok don't hurt Olivia I agree get Craig I agree with you. Bernie replied "great" see I knew you'd come around well Craig it is thanks Angel as if he wasn't just irate a few seconds ago. Angel is relieved that Bernie didn't hurt her some more. Bernie then says I'm going back into town see what's going on in the world then I'll see about Craig its lights out time for you I will see you later Angel. Angel yells wait!!!! Bernie stay here and keep me company please? Bernie replied that is what I got you the dog for Angel I'm a very busy man ok ill be back later. I remember the cops coming by early that next day to search Craig and I house for the first time. They were there for about an hour or so ripping through everything but in the end found absolutely nothing. Bernie was beginning to seem like he was untouchable I was drained and if I was I could only imagine how drained Detective Ross must have been. Then later that day Detective Ross called me and said that they have another break in the case that he had some great news that Craig and I should come to his office so we all could talk. He said that he had also called Anthony and that he was headed over now as well. So Craig and I jumped to it I kept saying to myself we are about to finally get this monster of a man. When Craig and I got to the police station Detective Ross greeted us in the lobby he looked so happy and thrilled that I could honestly say that I had never seen him like this before. Detective Ross escorted us into his office as we waited on Anthony to arrive Detective Ross then goes on to say listen I have some really good news as Anthony then walked through the door. Detective Ross says hello Anthony please take a seat as Craig and I both greeted him as well. The Detective goes on to say now upon reviewing all of the surveillance tapes I was able to get a break when Ralph's had a camera in their parking lot so the day Bernie came to see you Olivia I was able to get a view of a license plate number. Now the license plate wasn't a California plate it was an Arizona plate. Craig, Anthony, and I all at the same time said Arizona? Why would he have an Arizona plate? Detective Ross continued to say that's what I said to myself so I figured it was stolen maybe or something so I ran the plate and it comes up as a Frank Monroe. Now this is the license plate photo you all know what he looks like in person I've only seen him in black and white video is this Bernie the realtor? As all three of us looking at the photo in total shock and disbelief say "oh my god" yes that is him. Detective Ross says you all are 100% percent positive that this is him? We all replied at the same time yes that is him without a doubt that's him. Detective Ross says ok this is great. I replied ok well what happens next Detective? Detective Ross replied well we now have an address I'm going to Arizona to do what I do best that's all guys thank you for your time and help I will be in touch after I make an arrest. I said well where is Angel? Detective Ross replied Miss. Mathis I am on it. When Craig and I left out of Detective Ross office we spoke to Anthony outside for a few he just prayed that Angel was alive and ok and if so that Detective Ross can really find her. So the address that Detective Ross had was to a house in Phoenix at a 15161 Traverse lane so that was where Detective Ross was headed and I knew that this thing was either coming to an end or it was just getting started. Detective Ross flew out that way that next day after getting the plate number and checked into a near by hotel to stay for a few days casing the place before he actually made any kind of contact. He watched the place for an entire day 24 hours waiting to catch a glimpse of Bernie but he never showed up not even once. So now on day two of his investigation he sees a woman open the front door of the house and walk to the mailbox. I figured it was a girlfriend or something and a few minutes later two kids come up to the front door they must have been maybe ten and eleven or so. Detective Ross says to himself man it was time for me to do a bit more digging then make contact. Detective

Ross usually would park up the street on the opposite side of the road to see and look at the house from a distance. So finally when he dug enough he decided that it was time to go make official contact. Detective Ross got out of the rental car wearing dress pants and a dress shirt all black with a bulletproof vest underneath it all and his glock-9 handgun fully loaded behind his back walks across the street to the house and knocks on the front door. After about two knocks the woman response by saying who is it? The Detective says ma'm this is the police can you open the door please? The woman opens the door and says can I help you? Looking very confused as to why their was a cop knocking at her door for. Detective Ross replied by saying yes I hope you can help me as he then flashes her his badge and says my name is Detective Eris Ross I am a homicide Detective with the Los Angeles Police Department does a Frank Monroe live here ma'am? The woman says yes he does why do you ask? Detective Ross replied I'm sorry ma'am I didn't get your name you are? The woman replied by saying my name is Mary I am his wife what is this about Detective? You said you were a Los Angeles Detective this is Arizona? Detective Ross replied may I come in ma'am? Mary replied um sure let me just tell the kids to go to their rooms give me a second. As she let me through the front door I said ok sure ma'am this is a beautiful home you have here. Mary replied thank you Detective call me Mary please just have a seat give me a minute she says. Detective Ross says sure take your time as I see her whispering to a little boy then the boy and what I believed to be his brother go into a room and close the bedroom door behind them. Mary walks back to the living room where I was sitting she asks me

Detective can I get you anything? a glass of water? Tea? Coffee? Anything? Detective Ross replied by saying no I am fine thank you. Mary says are you sure? Its not a big deal I never have company it be nice for a change its always me and the kids as she finally takes a seat on the couch. Detective Ross replied yes I am sure, are we expecting your husband anytime soon Mary? Mary says "oh no" another week or so maybe at best my husband is an architect so he is never home always away on business. Mary then says so do you want to tell me why you are here for Detective? Detective Ross says Mary you don't watch the news at all? Mary replied by saying no my husband tells me that there is nothing on television but nonsense, negativity, and lies, so I watch movies that's all and what not. Detective Ross replied well I guess that makes sense given his current situation. Mary the reason that I am here is because your husband is the prime suspect in a murder and missing collage girls case he is wanted for murder and abduction Mary. Do you know where I can find him? Mary in total disbelief says what? What are you talking about? Frank a murderer? My husband wouldn't hurt a fly he is an architect not a murderer. Detective Ross replied Mary does the name Burke Walters ring a bell to you? Mary says yes he was a good man he died a few years ago why do you ask? Detective Ross says and did he go by the name Bernie? Who is he? Mary replied yes Burke was Franks foster parent for many years. Detective Ross says was he in real estate at all that you know of? Mary replied by saying yes he owned a few houses actually in Los Angeles when he died he gave all those homes to Frank. Detective Ross replied how many homes are their? And do you know exactly where these homes are located at? Mary replied by saying yes he owns three homes in Los Angeles and they are all on Circle street near UCLA what is going on Detective? Detective Ross also in total disbelief says "oh my god" Mary I need to find your husband how do you get in contact with him? Mary replied I call him or he calls me. Detective Ross says well can you call him now don't tell him that I am here though just tell him that you have an emergency and that you need him home. Mary replied by saying do you believe he really did these things Detective? Detective Ross replied I wouldn't be here if I didn't Mary the tapes don't lie hear you can watch them yourself here are even photos from places where he stalks these student. Mary we are running out of time Frank has killed one girl already, assaulted another, and another is still missing. Detective Ross continues to say listen I will leave this stuff here with you as he places three tapes on her coffee table with an envelope with still shots in it and says I will go now look over that all then you decide if you want to make that call. The choice is yours Mary don't allow your husband to hurt anyone else its clear he hasn't been honest even with you. Mary replied ok let me go over this stuff first Detective please with a look of confusion on her face. Detective Ross replied by saying sure here is my card Mary call me I'm in town another few days that's all and Detective Ross left. As soon as he got back into his car he got a trace put onto Mary Monroe's phone because he had no idea weather Mary was in on this or not and even if she wasn't odds are she will still help her husband. From the hotel he would listen in on Mary's phone calls all night but not one call made from her to Bernie and not one call made into her as well. That next morning Detective Ross went back to

Mary's house and knocked on the door. A little kid opened the front door and says mom a guy is at the door!!! as I say well hello their young man what's your name? the little boy replied by saying I'm not allow to talk to strangers. Detective Ross says that is absolutely correct you shouldn't your parents taught you well. As Mary came to the door and said Frank go to your room please and what did I tell you about opening the front door? The little boy says sorry mom and ran to his room. Mary says sorry about that Detective come on in she said. As the Detective walks in he says quickly so are we making this call now? Mary replied yes right now as she begins to dial Bernie's phone number. Ring, ring, ring nobody answered as Mary leaves a voice message saying hey honey can you please call me back as soon as you can I have an emergency here at the house thank you and hung up the phone. Then Mary says their you "happy" now? Detective Ross replied no not yet I'm not when he answers I will be. Then about five or ten minutes later as I waited around Mary's phone rings and its her husband and Detective Ross tells her to answer and keep him or the phone. Mary answers the phone and says hey honey? Bernie replied all casually by saying hey babe I just got your message I'm sorry I didn't answer I'm so tied up with work what's wrong babe? how are you and the boys doing? Mary replied I'm very sick honey I don't feel good I need to go to the hospital can you come home? Bernie replied yeah babe can you give me one more day just to wrap this project up? Mary replied yes that is fine honey just hurry up please. Bernie says I will what's wrong you sound different, worried, or something? Mary replied no honey just feeling sick not like myself that's all. Bernie replied ok babe I will be home soon sit tight I love you very much you and the boys you know that right? Everything I do is for you all. Mary replied I know Frank I love you too see you soon honey. Bernie replied see you soon babe and hung up. Mary then says there are you happy now? He is on his way? Detective Ross in a rush says thank you Mary I have to go I'll talk to you soon as he jets out the door in a hurry. Mary looking confused hurries to pick back up the phone. Detective Ross on the phone with another officer says hey did you trace the call? The officer replied yes Detective Ross but this is so weird it comes up that he is at UCLA sir. Detective Ross replied what the fuck? Listen get units over there now !!!!! and find that piece of shit now!!!! The officer replied ok boss I'm on it now. As Detective Ross goes to start his car he gets a call on his cell phone from Mary as Mary says Detective who is the young woman in the video that my husband is talking to in the grocery store? Detective Ross replied by saying that is a young collage student who your husband is stalking, he also assaulted her once before why do you ask Mary? Mary says "oh my lord" I recognize this girl. Detective Ross says recognize her how Mary? Mary replied what is her name Detective? Detective Ross says you know I cant tell you that Mary now how do you recognize her? Mary says well Detective if you cant tell me her name then why should I tell you how I recognize her? Detective Ross says ok Mary her name is Olivia now your turn? Mary replied Olivia what Detective? Detective Ross replied Mathis now how do you recognize her? Now Mary? Mary replied by saying "wow" I knew it my husband and I went to UCLA many years ago this is how he and I first met. She continues yep their was this girl that he was obsessed with her name was Nicole Mathis she never wanted Frank no matter how hard he tried nothing he did was ever good enough it broke poor Franks heart. But in the end I guess he settled for me the three of us were all in Professor Lucas's class he loved theater and wanted to be an actor so anyways that girl that he is stalking is Nicole's daughter. Detective Ross replied wait did you just say Professor Lucas's class? Mary says yes my husbands favorite teacher he took it hard when the Professor passed away. Detective Ross replied he is dead? Does he have a son that you know of? Mary replied no he never had any kids that I knew of. Detective Ross says ok and you are sure that Olivia is Nicole's daughter? Mary replied I'm positive. The detective says ok thank you very much Mary but I have to go ill be in touch and the detective hung up on her then he immediately called Olivia. I answered and said hello Detective any good news yet? In a rush and panic Detective Ross says Olivia I don't have much time what is your mothers name he asked? I said my mothers name? Detective Ross replied yes what is her name? I said her name is Nicole why? Detective Ross replied by saying have you seen Bernie on campus at all today? I replied no why? Detective Ross says never mind I have to go I will talk to you soon as I say wait hold up!!!! But the detective hung up on me. Detective Ross gets on the phone with the officer whom he had spoke to before in Los Angeles and says get to UCLA now!!!! find Professor Lucas he is the Professor I repeat Bernie is the Professor go now !!!!!!! Hurry up!!!! Find this cocksucker I have no time to explain just get to the theater I'm driving back to Los Angeles now go!!!!! And hung up. As Detective Ross peels out of the neighborhood and jumps on the highway sirens and all with his windows down yells move!!!!! Move!!!!!. Mary picks up the phone again this time to call her husband to tell him what was going on. Bernie answered the phone right away this time and said baby this is really not a good time I will be home soon can I call you back? Mary replied by saying don't bother I'm sure you are busy stalking young collage girls huh? What did you think I wouldn't find out? Yes Detective Ross of the fucking Los Angeles Police Department was here at our home Frank where our children sleep you pig what do you have to say now hotshot? Mary continues Nicole's daughter? Are you that obsessed with her Frank? Bernie replied baby you don't know what you are talking about its not what you think. Now what did you tell that cop? Mary replied by saying "oh I told him everything" you stay the fuck away from me and the kids you sick fuck I saw the tapes and pictures Frank. Bernie replied baby don't believe that. baby that's all bullshit you know the alter these things and what not I'm on my way home now will talk about it honey. Mary says the fact that you think I believe your bullshit is crazy so yeah we will talk about divorce and a restraining order that's what will talk about. Listen Bernie said your not taking my kids and your not leaving me the only way you leave me is dead. Bernie continues to say now I'm trying to remain calm you need to as well Mary ok? Mary replied fuck you Frank go to hell. As Bernie still very calmly says Mary I forbid you to hang up this phone on me. As Mary hangs up all Bernie hears is a dial tone. Bernie in rage now turns around and looks at Angel and says you fucking whore you really think your going to leave me? and take my fucking kids away? I will kill you bitch as he picks up a knife. Angel begins to scream Bernie no!!!!! what the fuck are you talking about????? I don't have your kids???? Bernie yells shut the fuck up bitch!!!!! I loved you!!!!!! I did everything for you!!!!! And this is how you repay me???? With this dark twisted look of rage in his face he grabs Angel by the back of her head as Angel is yelling no!!!!!!! Bernie slit Angels throat as blood squirted everywhere and then began to stab her in the chest repeatedly over and over and over again multiple times as he is yelling why did you do this to me????? I loved you!!!!!!!! As he continues to stab Angels lifeless body. As Bernie begins to snap out of his rage he then talks to Angels mutilated body and says well Angel I have to go I'm sorry. Bernie then turns around kicks the door to this room open as he begins to run down a long semi lit hallway as fast as he can saying to himself what the fuck have you done ????? Once Bernie gets to the end of this musty semi lit hallway he then walks up a few stairs then opens up a door above his head there is a dark area then he opens two cabinet doors and crawls out from underneath a sink it appears that he is in a bathroom when he finally stands up. Bernie continues to walk out of the bathroom as he opens up the bathroom door and continues down a hallway through the living room as a young black male sat in a chair watching television gets out of the chair because he heard someone walking in his house. It is Anthony as he then sees Bernie in his living room and says "what the fuck" what are you doing in my house? Bernie replied by saying I'm leaving and shot Anthony right between his eyes and continued to walk right out the front door like it was nothing to him. Bernie then walks out the house and walks down the street to a black four door BMW he jumps in the car starts it up and speeds down the street and heads for the highway. Officer Stockton who works very close with Detective Ross had just been pulling up on campus and heard the shot go off as he then pushed it faster parked his squad car and ran up on campus as fast as he could as he yells to students get down!!!!! Running down to Professor Lucas's classroom. A squad truck pulled up right after with a dozen Los Angeles Police officers squared up all in tactical gear with fingers on triggers locked and loaded looking for Bernie. When the officers finally get to Professor Lucas's classroom as they kick in the door the Professor is nowhere to be found so Officer Stockton then calls Detective Ross as Detective Ross picks up and says did you get the son of a bitch yet? Officer Stockton replied no sir I got about a dozen guys here we are searching his classroom as well as the entire campus. He continues to say also boss a shot went off as I was pulling up he is defiantly here where the fuck is this guy? He is not in this classroom Eric? Detective Ross replied find him Stockton he is there we need to put this shit to bed tonight you hear me? Officer Stockton replied yes I hear you sir I'm on it sir. Detective Ross says I'm on my way but I'm far away even if I flew I wouldn't make it there on time so I'm going to need you to catch this prick make it happen as he hung up the phone. Then just as Officer Stockton was getting off of the phone with Detective Ross another officer yells over to Stockton officer Stockton!!!! I got something here!!!!! You might want to come over here and check this out. Officer Stockton looks over and says what do you got for me???? It better be good the Detective wants this handled today. The officer says well we searched the entire room and everything looked on the up and up until I noticed a latch underneath the Professors desk with a throw rug over it. He continues so I lifted the carpet up and it appears to be a door of some sort maybe to a basement or something like that I didn't go in or anything I cracked it open a bit but that's about it sir. Officer Stockton says what?? Let me see this as he follows the officer to the Professors desk as he looks for himself. Officer Stockton in compete disbelief says what the fuck is this??? As he lifted the door open. It was a dark hole that was it just very scary looking. So Officer Stockton decided to give Detective Ross a call to see what they should do about it. Detective Ross picked up the phone and said you got him? Officer Stockton replied no but we got something here Eric listen is there any basement at UCLA whatsoever? Detective Ross says no why? Officer Stockton replied ok because the Professor here has a hidden door here underneath his desk with a latch and a throw rug on top of it. Detective Ross says ok what is it? Officer Stockton said I'm not sure yet sir. Detective Ross said well quietly get your men down there and check it out now!!!!! What are you waiting for???? Officer Stockton replied yes sir we are on it. After officer Stockton hung up he ordered his men to get ready that they were all going down there. So officer Stockton told the officer who found the door to open it and lead the way as he already broke the lock that was on it. So as he opened the floor door they pointed a flash light down there and saw stairs leading to the floor. Then officer Stockton said fuck it I will go first the rest of you follow me. Officer Stockton then turns around and begins to step down the stairs on the way down he sees a light switch. Officer Stockton is the first man in and says quietly "I found a switch" he hits it and on come a long hallway filled with Christmas lights as Officer Stockton says "holy shit" what the fuck is this place? As the rest of the officers come down in complete disbelief with guns all pointed down the hallway. The officers begin quietly walking down this long hallway that is completely empty as they continue down the hallway they come up on a door one to the left of them with another above there head. Officer Stockton tells his men that he is going up to the one above their heads to see what it is. As officer Stockton walks up the stairs he opens up the door and sees nothing it is pitch black but only a tiny light coming through so he pushes two small cabinet doors open and sees that he is in a bathroom. Officer Stockton crawls through the cabinet and into the bathroom floor as he stands up and points his gun at a closed bathroom door. On his walkie talkie he tells two officers to come up as the rest stay in the hallway. The two officers come up as Officer Stockton quietly opens the bathroom door and proceeds to search the house. After a thro search all three officers say "The house is clear" once again in total disbelief officer Stockton says to himself "son of a bitch" this is Clarence Johnson's house. As the other two officers look so confused as to what they are seeing Officer Stockton says this son of a bitch has been tunneling into these homes holy shit I have to tell Ross now. On the phone with Detective Ross Officer Stockton says Detective this guy has been tunneling into these homes I'm standing in Clarence Johnsons home right now Detective and I got here from Professor Lucas's desk at UCLA this fucking guy has been one step ahead of us the entire time sir. Detective Ross replied son of a bitch that's how Clarence got that bullet hole Bernie that sick fuck shot him after he already took his own life. He continues this also explains why Maria Coopers body was found in the Professors classroom Bernie is Professor Lucas he is a film student he is wearing a disguise we had him right in front of us this whole entire time and didn't even know it he has been playing with us all along. He goes on to say continue looking we need to find this guy we will get him trust me on that. Officer Stockton replied ok Detective I'm going to continue the search. Officer Stockton then ordered his men to go back into the tunnel now they go into the other room as Officer Stockton kicks in that door and flicks on the lights he sees a room with only a chair with straps and a table with weapons of all sorts guns, bats, knives, etc. their was also blood splatter on the wall but still no sign of Bernie whatsoever. The team backs out of the room and continues down the hallway some more and yet again come across another door to the left and another above them. Officer Stockton then kicks in the door to the left as his team rushes in they find pictures all over of Olivia Mathis also another chair with straps and a table of weapons but still no sign of Bernie though. Officer Stockton then goes up through the door above them and its another bathroom sink door as Stockton is trying to be very quiet he hears the sound of a television playing. Officer Stockton opens up the bathroom door very slowly as his team follows closely behind him. Officer Stockton hears a woman's voice from within the kitchen he then cocks his glock9 back and yells "freeze" as he jumps from around the corner scaring the woman half to death he then realizes that its Olivia Mathis as she screams very loud and says how in the hell did you get into my house??????? Officer Stockton replies ma'am Los Angeles

Police Department my name is Officer Stockton there is no need to be alarmed I'm sorry to startle you I need to call Detective Ross right away and then I will explain ma'am. Officer Stockton then calls the Detective and says ok Eric my team and I walked further down the tunnel and the same thing sir another door above us and to the left of us I am in the door above us now and it lead me into another bathroom only this time I am in Olivia Mathis's house. Detective Ross says so this guy tunnels into the homes that he owns. He sold all these homes for this purpose solely we are dealing with one sick fuck. What is in the other room officer? Officer Stockton replied checking that room next sir but still no sign of Bernie sir. Another thing that room sir was like a room blacked out with a chair with straps attached to it in it and a table with weapons on it in there we also noticed blood splatter on walls and floor sir. Olivia then replied "that's it" as Officer Stockton said excuse me? Olivia says that's the room he had me in "oh my god" that is why he kept telling me that I was home because I was underneath my own house. Officer Stockton said it's your call Detective what do you want me to do? Detective Ross replied you keep going find him you said you heard a gun go off he is there find him. As for Miss. Mathis you need to leave home now or keep two officers with her while you continue your search I'm on my way go now!!!!!! Hurry!!!!!!. Officer Stockton replied ok sir we are on it. Miss. Mathis I'm leaving two officers here unless you want to leave he asked me? I said no sir my boyfriend wants us to stay here. Officer Stockton replied where is your boyfriend now? I said he is at practice sir. Officer Stockton replied ok as he tells his two men behind him to stay here until the search is over as both men say ok sir. Officer Stockton goes back down into the tunnel as the rest of his team awaited him. He says guys move out!!!!! Lets get this other door open!!!!! As his men kick open the other door to the left open only to find the same type of room an all black room with a wooden chair with straps attached to it and a side table of weapons. This was the cleanest room so far like he hadn't even used this one yet before which we found to be very weird. As the team approaches the end of this tunnel there is one more room to the left of us and the last door above our heads. Officer Stockton orders his team to kick in the side door first and once we hit the lights there was blood everywhere. There is a young lady sitting strapped to a chair covered in blood with her head down missing fingers, ear, you name it. This was the sickest thing Officer Stockton and his team had every seen it was something out of a horror movie just horrific it smelled horrible. Officer Stockton called Detective Ross and says Eric we have a mutilated body here of a young woman I think this is your girl here sir this shit is very bad. Detective Ross replied fuck!!!!!! Yes that has to be Angel Clause. Son of a bitch !!!!!!! Call the coroner where the fuck is this guy?????? Officer Stockton says ok will do sir but still no sign of him and I have men all over this entire campus and we are in this tunnel at the end I only have one more door to check sir I'm going to get up there and then I will call you ok? Detective Ross replied yeah ok. Officer Stockton then crawled up the next door as his men secured the area. Officer Stockton yelled down to his team we got something up here boys another bathroom!!!!!!! I'm going in be right back!!!!!!. As Officer Stockton crawls through the bathroom sink and into the bathroom only this time the bathroom door was cracked open as Officer Stockton gets to his feet quietly then draws his weapon slowly he yells is anybody here?????? Los Angeles Police Department I am armed he says. With no response Officer Stockton ripped open the door and walks down the hallway turns into the kitchen area then continues to the living room. There he sees a black male laid out on the floor blood everywhere still yet again no sign of Bernie. Officer Stockton yells to his team "I got one" then calls Detective Ross as Ross answers quickly saying please tell me that you have good news for me???? Officer Stockton replied by saying no sir none at all I'm sorry but not only did we find Angel Clause I now just found Anthony Jones but I do know where that gun shot came from now. This guy was just here but he is gone now we went through the entire tunnel sir. You were right sir he has been using the collage to tunnel into all three homes how did we miss this sir? Detective Ross replied I don't know man I don't know but listen get out there now and ask neighbors because if you heard the shot then someone else did as well find him or her and ask some questions now!!!! And he hung up the phone. As the team came up from the tunnel Officer Stockton walked outside of Anthony Jones's house to see what he could find out. At this point their were a dozen cops outside and people as well one guy who lived down the street said he saw a man run out of Anthony's house wearing all black and that he jumped into an all black BMW and peeled out soon after he heard the gun shot go off. This was the tip we needed as I called the Detective to tell him the news I said Eric I'm here right now with a neighbor that saw a man wearing all black leaving Anthony's house right after the gun shot went off he also can identify the vehicle that the suspect drove off in and it was a 1995 BMW all black sir. Detective Ross replied by saying "holy shit" that's him and that's his car I know the plates get an APB put out on this plate number right now!!!! 1085-WBS and call me once its done Detective Ross said. Officer Stockton said ok boss I'm on it click. As Detective Ross is still speeding as fast as he can trying to make it back to Los Angeles he gets a call back from Officer Stockton. Detective Ross answers the phone flying down 1-10 and says tell me something good officer? Officer Stockton very pleased with himself says yes sir we spotted the vehicle he is on the San Bernardino Fwy headed towards home I'm guessing sir. Detective Ross yelling where????? Where????? I'm on the same fucking highway I need an exact location on this prick hurry up!!!!! Officer Stockton says hold on sir I'm checking now. Officer Stockton still on the phone with Detective Ross radios to dispatch I need exact location on a BMW plate number 1085-WBS on the San Bernardino Fwy? Dispatch radios back sir we have him at between Lexington and Vermont. Officer Stockton continued to say Eric your guy is on San Bernardino Fwy between Lexington and Vermont headed in the opposite direction from you sir. As Detective Ross replied that's a 10/4 and whipped his car around over the median and all saying to himself I got you now mother fucker, your ass is mine. As Detective Ross began speeding as fast as he could sirens blaring as he yells out the windows move!!!!! Move people!!!!! Detective Ross calls back Officer Stockton and says direct me am I close or not???? Stockton replied no sir you are about 10 miles behind him now sir. After several miles Detective Ross finally catches up with the black BMW he tells dispatch, officer Stockton, and all, to fall back with helicopters and all that because he didn't want to draw attention to Bernie he wanted Bernie to feel like he got away. Once Detective Ross finally caught up to Bernie he stayed right behind him for a few more miles as Bernie just continued to drive straight at regular speed as if he had no care in the world what so ever. Then Detective Ross told dispatch and Officer Stockton ok I'm about to pull him over here now but right as he said this Bernie began to veer off to the next exit. So Detective Ross says wait!!! What the fuck is this guy doing??? He is getting off at an exit. Detective Ross continues to say I'm going to follow him some more see where he is going as Officer Stockton and dispatch all await in anticipation. Bernie pulls off of the highway and pulls up to what appears to be a warehouse. Bernie pulls up to the front entrance of the warehouse and came to a complete stop and turns off the car. Clearly at this point he sees Detective Ross through his rear view mirror but just sat there he didn't even get out of the car whatsoever not a single movement even made by him from within the car. But what I did notice was that through his rearview mirror he was staring dead right at me but at this point I was starring right back at him as well. Once Detective Ross opens his car door Bernie then opens his as well as Detective Ross yelled come out with your hands up Bernie it's over!!!!!!!! Bernie replied by saying that's not going to happen Detective but I will come out with my loaded gun and aim it at your head that sounds better what do you say Detective? Detective Ross says come on Bernie or should I say Frank nobody else needs to die. Bernie replied by saying you think your so clever, so smart, huh? Your very pleased with yourself? You didn't find anything that I didn't want you to find Detective trust me when I tell you that. Detective Ross says put the gun down Bernie and step out of the car. I'm putting mine down on the floor here outside the car so you can see it and then I'm stepping out of my vehicle can you do the same? Bernie replied by saying no that is where your wrong Detective someone else does have to die here today and its you this will be your final resting place. As Bernie then steps out of the vehicle with a loaded hand gun pointed right at Detective Ross's head Detective Ross drops down and shoots Bernie right in the chest about three times as Bernie fires off one shot that hit Detective Ross in the arm. As Detective Ross tries to get himself back up in pain off of the floor he looks over and sees Bernie laid out outside of his car door. Detective Ross then calls dispatch for help while he then calls officer Stockton to tell him that "its over" I got him he said as the whole squad team cheers over the speaker phone. Officer Stockton says is he dead? Detective Ross says yes he is dead. Then Detective Ross hangs up his cell phone gets out of the car to walk over to Bernie and says to himself what the fuck???? As he realizes that Bernie's body was gone. Detective Ross now looking under Bernie's car waving his gun around in total disbelief that he is gone yells Bernie!!!!!!! Detective Ross runs into the warehouse yelling Bernie where the fuck are you??????? Bernie nowhere to be found Detective Ross calls dispatch and yells find him!!!!!! He got away!!!! Officer Stockton calls Detective Ross saying I thought you said that he was dead sir? Detective Ross yells I though he was I fucking shot him like three times in the chest he was laid the fuck out what the fuck he yells find him he couldn't have gotten that far. As Detective Ross and other local deputies search the entire area there was no sign of him almost as if he vanished into thin air. A local fisherman said that there was nothing out there but this closed down warehouse and a boat dock behind the warehouse so unless he swam I have no idea where he would be Detective. The chief of police came out and asked Detective Ross why he didn't check his pulse? Then told the Detective that he will be in hot water for that mishap then told him to go to the hospital and get his arm looked at. The chief then said now get out of here I will clean up this mess the press is going to have a field day with this one Detective. Detective Ross walked away pissed the fuck off as he sat there and thought to himself why here he said? Why did he come to this warehouse? This spot? Why? Bernie is a very calculated guy he wouldn't have come to this exact location for no reason at all. Why here??????..........................ONE YEAR LATER MIAMI FLORIDA. Two young ladies in a Publix grocery store are shopping on this hot beautiful Miami day. They go into the check out line as one of the pretty woman says to her friend girl I'm so tired of living on campus we need to get ourselves an apartment we need our own place what do you think about that? The other girl says I agree 100% percent lets do it. A man in the grocery store line behind the young women wearing a black suit and tie says hey ladies I don't mean to ease drop but I couldn't help but over hear that you all are looking for an apartment? One of the girls replied that's totally rude and creepy but yeah we are why do you know of any places? The gentleman says I'm sorry didn't mean to be rude I'm actually a landlord out here this is my card give me a call sometime. The other girl whispers to her friend girl he is cute and totally hitting on you take it girl. She says girl stop as she replied to the gentleman sorry about my friend sure I will sometime my name is Claire by the way. The gentleman replied its ok its nice to meet you Claire my name is Eric, Eric Ross. The girl says oh cool like that Detective that went crazy when he couldn't find that realtor in California? The gentleman replied g I guess so come to think about it. As all three of them laughed the gentleman continues to say well you all have a nice day as he walked away he smiled with a sadistic grin.

THE END

GETTING SCHOOL'D

a poem by:
May'lon "Maze" Miranda

Getting School'd
all throughout my youth I was considered a fool.
cause I didn't do what they did or believed in what they do
they always went RIGHT and I always chose LEFT.
all they could say was he a fuckin mess. But the kid dress code
mad fresh and on the black top ya boy was the best.
I told em that I was gonna be the greatest and that was before
I even knew I was. I want yall to thank ALI for that.
in fact thank MALCOLM thank MAYA ANGELOU
thank B.I.G. and thank PAC for that.
MARTIN had a DREAM and like him I did too.
PUFF and RUSSELL on the wall oh he a fag for that or he
slow, he lazy, ask DRE bout STEPHIN FETCHIT like that.
but sticks and stones never broke my bones lock my body can't
trap my mind ask HOV about that.
Even when I did wrong my heart remind pure I thank GOD
and the LIFE lessons, JAIL, and all for my WIFE my KIDS
for you all I STAND TALL.

THANK YOU'S

First off I want to thank my lord and savior Jesus Christ for without him none of this would be possible. I want to thank my beautiful wife for standing by my side no matter what the situation may be. you truly are my best friend we have been through so much together and I'm glad that I get to share life's journey with a woman as strong, smart, and, beautiful as you I love you Jess. I want to thank my eldest son May'lon and his brothers Shawn, Ja'Sir, Malakai, you all are my inspiration and motivation biological or not I miss you all and hope and pray you all grow up to be strong, healthy, and, successful young men I'm always here for you all daddy loves yall to death. Thank you to the New Port Richey Public Library for all the love and support over the years thank you to Ron Baylow, Aamco, and to my father in-law Ernesto "Classic Man" Rios, Eddie Rios, Melissa Marangos-Rios, Catches water front grille, The homie Manuel "Jr" Aguirre, Samuel "Jersey Boy" Devault, Inbox Dollars, Amazon, Books-a-million, Barnes and Noble, Ebay, Becky Hardy, Aj Hardy, Josh Muffitt, Jeremy Hodgkiss, The entire Miranda family, The entire Almonds family, Special shout out to my Aunt barbara for everything you saved my life. to my brother Dashaune thank you bro for all of your help throughout the years you drive me crazy but you my brother for life yo badboyz4Life. Thank you also to George "The Duke" Rollins, My guys Andre Potts, John "Bswag" Beeman, Chris "Righteous" Dorsey my brother from another, Tattoo guys Maan Nelson, Will DeSimone, AirBrush Mike for holding down my clothing line, Tyrone and Glenda, Amy Fazzi and her fam much luv, The homie Terrence good looks on that gig bro you too also saved my life, ya brother Curt and ya moms Sheila I got mad luv for yall real talk. my guy Neil even though we ain't spoke in a hot minute thanks for all the advice and good times. to my brother Evan Jenkins I'm glad we got to reconnect love you bro, Mirza and Rick I could never apologize enough for what I did years ago but I have grown so much and I hope you both have seen that I love yall, every outlet or store that sells my shit, all my Facebook family and followers, all my Twitter followers, all my Instagram followers I love all yall much love. The best for last THANK YOU TO LOUIS AND ANNA MIRANDA everything I do is to make you all proud of me because everyday I am proud to call myself your son. I know you both are smiling down on me from heaven see you both again when I get there I love you both so much. if I missed anybody or forgot anybody please don't be upset with me I just know entirely way to many people.

I LOVE ALL YALL
UNO

- Author May'lon "Maze" Miranda

P.S. This is my 5th ring why stop now........ the sky is the limit.

If you enjoyed The Realtor
look for more titles at www.maylonmiranda.com also
Follow us on the web at www.facebook.com/loveisblindbook123
www.facebook.com/TheRealMainSuspect and www.
facebook.com/mirandapublishingllc also on
Twitter @Maylon Miranda
Instagram @ author.maylon.miranda
Youtube @ Maylon Miranda

MIRANDA PUBLISHING

BONUS POEM

SUCCESS

By
May'lon "Maze" Miranda

Nobody can see it but me/
Nobody else can hear it but me/
I can see it but I'm not there yet/
I can feel it but I cant touch it/
I have tunnel vision I see how it will all play out without a
Doubt/ for every five steps that I get closer to it/ it feels like I
Get kicked back about ten/ throughout the journey I lost a lot of
Friends but that's ok because throughout all the heartache and
Pain I picked up the pen/ I want it so bad for me and my ken/
I will see it out till the very end for it is my destiny I've said
This time and time again/ there is not one person alive who can
Stop me but me I must see it through until the very end/ the
Finish line awaits I have children that depend on me I cant be
Late/ for all you haters wishing on my down fall take a seat
With the rest and wait/ it will never happen its what drives me
This is my fate/ SUCCESS I will have it no matter what it
Takes.

Printed in the United States
By Bookmasters